Hugh Schpenus Trilogy

The Greatest Schpenus Story Ever Told

Prologue

What started as a simple breakfast conversation became a short story written in a day. What started as a single story soon developed into an entirely unexpected trilogy! Now, here we are with a printed version containing all three Hugh Schpenus books together. These three stories are intended to be read and seen as an eighties B-Movie action-comedy.

Follow Hugh Schpenus as he travels throughout the world, all while trying to save the day! I dedicate this novel to my wife, Peggy Luna. She suggested the name for the starring role and the overall idea and concept. I copyrighted the name instantly after realizing how ingenious of a name it is! I am grateful to have such a supportive woman in my life. Thank you, Carlos L. Diaz, for designing such an amazing cover. Your incredible creativity has taken this novel to a new level! Angelica Polis, thank you so much for proofreading all three stories! Oleg, my friend, I dedicate this book to you as well for inspiring me with book three! And thank you, my fantastic reader, for taking the time to read this. I dedicate this to you as well. I seriously hope you enjoy this epic story as much as I have enjoyed writing it.

Hugh Schpenus Goes Undercover

Crime doesn't pay, and sometimes it takes a special kind of man to show why.

Chapter 1

VHS

Here I am, running down the street after another criminal. A criminal who thinks they could get away with their crimes. Little do they know they are messing with the wrong detective. Whoever crosses the line of crime must deal with me. Hugh Schpenus. My name is unique, I know. A little about me: I am Austrian, and I live in a dangerous city known as West End. It's in a state that I like to call the state of Confusion because people who come here end up on the wrong side of the law, which confuses me. Why? Because why try to commit crimes when a hardnose detective is here?

I have a black belt in Aikido and Tang Soo Do. No one can get past these iron hands. Do you think the Great Wall is great? You haven't tried to cross over the Hugh Schpenus. I am the real deal here.

Take this guy in front of me. Running down the street thinking he's a cheetah, but I can hear him huffing and puffing like a fat rhino. My legs of speed have gained traction. I am catching up to him like a Shinkansen running two minutes late. Like the Japanese bullet train, Hugh Schpenus is never behind schedule.

I am sure you're wondering what this criminal did to cross paths with me. I will tell you. He stole something. Others will say it was a petty theft crime, but I will say that any crime is big in my book. The book of Schpenus. I grabbed the thick handle of his backpack and yanked him back like a magnet against a block of steel. He lost his footing thanks to my Hugh strength. The bag ripped, and out went the evidence: Fifteen adult films. VHS. Yeah, I got myself another bag. Case closed. Crime solved. The Hugh Schpenus way.

The X-rated box covers fell into a nearby pothole filled with a mixture of dirty rainwater and regret. The temptation of the skin teased my eyes, but I stayed focused on the criminal on the floor. He looked like a real class A pervert, too. You know the type. Combover, beady eyes, and the fifty-year-old thick mustache. Maybe this guy is lonely, I don't know, but he broke the law, and now he must pay.

"You have the right to remain silent," I declared.

The man looked up at me, wide-eyed and still in shock.

"Yeah, I got you. Now make this easy on yourself, punk."

"Look, man, I am sorry. Can you at least give me a warning? I can't go back."

I chuckled. A car showed up with two beat cops.

"You should have thought of that before you stepped foot into that video store. Lesson learned crime doesn't pay."

I cuffed him without resistance.

"No, listen, man, listen!" He frantically yelled at me. "If you let me go, I will tell you a secret."

"Secret? Hugh Schpenus has no secrets."

"Wait, what? What's your name?"

I answered him with silence and tossed him into the back of the squad car.

"I am glad you showed up just in time," I said while lighting a cigarette to calm my nerves.

The male cop sighed and shook his head at me. "Let me guess, you got yourself another 'fish in the bag,' huh Schpenus?"

"You're damn right I did!" I said to him in my trademarked aggressive tone.

The female cop chuckled, "Come on, Frank, let's get out of here."

After the cops left, I grabbed the evidence and headed back to my office. Another late night of paperwork. That's the worst part of all this. After the action is done, I have to write a report on all of this. Hugh has no time to write about the crime happening out there.

The night is still young. Passion still lingers in the air. The desire for more crime to unfold. And when it does. I, Hugh Schpenus, will be right here waiting.

Chapter 2

Relax Schpenus Relax

My boss was reading the police report in front of me. His eyes darted from side to side as if I wrote some sort of biography on my entire life. I smiled to myself. If I wrote one of those, it would be a bestseller. People would demand a movie, and I would pick one of those fantastic action stars to play me. Think about it. Seeing a famous action star on the big screen chasing down criminals. Hugh Schpenus is on the big screen. I can't imagine seeing a story about my life as a movie. It sounds too good to be true.

I suppose this is an excellent time to tell you about my life.

I was born in Bad Ischl, Austria. I came here to be a bodybuilder, but instead, I fell into a life of combatting crime. My sensei John Action Kaminski suggested it, and it was the best advice I have ever received. Aside from becoming this muscular mastodon that strikes fear in the heart of criminals when they look upon me. I am thirty-five years old, which means I am in my optimal prime.

"Hugh," my boss said while clasping his hands together on his desk. His fifty-year-old face showed a history of witnessing crime and punishment. "I know you like to work alone, but you're getting tasked with a partner for this next assignment. I want you to be nice to him, he's a bit fresh in this world, and I want you to show him the ropes."

"Stacy," I said while shaking my head in disagreement.

He held his hand up and stopped me, "I know what you are going to say; you work alone."

"Yeah! That's right, I work alone. You know what happened to my last partner."

My last partner was killed in the line of duty. We were out rescuing a survivor from a burning building when an elderly woman pleaded with my partner to save her chihuahua, Pico. He was rescued, but at the cost of my partner's life.

"His name is Carl White. He's like you, a trained fighter. He's heard a great deal about you and wants to learn from you. So please, show him the ropes and be nice to him, okay?"

I shook my head in disgust, "Okay, fine."

Just then, the door opened, and Carl walked in. To my surprise, he was not what I expected.

"Hi, I am," as he held out his hand, I stood up and greeted him.

"Carl, I heard. My name is," but before I could complete my sentence, he cut me off.

"Hugh, Hugh Schpenus. Yeah, I know who you are," he said with an excited grin. "I heard a lot about you."

I smiled at him. Maybe I was too quick to judge my new partner. He looked tough, too. Almost my height, which means at 5'7, 250lbs of pure muscle, I was looking at a formidable ally. Sure, he may not be as muscular as I am, but he looked tough.

"Can you two take the bromance somewhere else? I have a lot of work to do here. Your assignments are on your desk," ordered Stacy.

"Sure, sorry, boss," I responded.

Carl and I returned to our desks where I found a long envelope.

"Looks like our desks are right by each other, huh?" he declared.

I smiled at him after hearing his enthusiasm and nodded.

"Come on," I said to him. "Let's go and get a coffee and chat. I would like to get to know who I will be working with before we go out in the field."

I was just as excited and enthusiastic as Carl, but I tried my best to stay cool, calm, and collected.

After we grabbed our coffees in the breakroom, we sat down at one of the small circular tables. The break room was empty, which was good since we could talk without anyone hearing us.

"So, tell me about you, Carl. Where are you from?"

He took a sip of his coffee and then lowered the Styrofoam cup onto the table.

"I am originally from Korea, but I was adopted and moved to Idaho. Of all places I know, it doesn't sound too exciting. My parents were the cliché potato farmers, but I craved something more. I studied boxing and karate at a local gym. After graduating from the university, I decided to move down here. Luckily, there was a spot for me to be a detective here. As soon as I heard I was going to be your partner, well," he smiled. "The rest is history."

A smile crossed my face, "That's great to hear. You heard about me?"

He took another sip and nodded his head, "Oh yeah, Hugh, I heard about the big drug bust you did two years ago."

"Ah, yeah," I replied. "That was over in the shipping yard back in '85. Yeah, I remember that day."

"Where are you from? Let me guess? Austria?" Carl asked, lowering his cup.

I laughed aloud, "How did you know my accent? It is quite thick, they say."

He laughed, "It does remind me of that action movie star. He came out with a new movie recently about him traveling through time or something."

"Ah yeah, I saw that movie. It was a good role despite the character not being Austrian."

"Yeah, he did play the role very well."

"I hear there's a sequel coming up where he is in space or something," I said while finishing the last of my coffee. "Okay, come on now, let's get back to our desks and talk shop. It's time to get down to business."

Chapter 3

Belinda the Beast

"Okay, so it says here we're going after this Guatemalan crime lord named Carlos Dirty Sanchez," I state while looking at his profile dossier. He is forty-five years old, short, stocky, and has a black mustache. He shouldn't be too hard to find since he's balding and lives over in the Diamond Coastal area."

"We should do some reconnaissance beforehand," suggested Carl.

"Oh, what do you mean like undercover?"

He nodded at my question.

"Hmm, I say we drive over there and take a look around. Maybe grab a bite to eat, too. I am hungry, yeah."

"Good idea. I know a good taco stand over there. Stanley's Sexy Snacking Tacos."

I laughed, "That's a mouthful right there! Let's go!"

Outside, the summer heat was beating down on us like an angry mother with a leather belt; we approached my car.

"Whoa! Sweet ride? What is this, a sixty-seven?" Carl asked while admiring my black muscle car.

"Yeah, I like to take this out whenever I go undercover. This car can haul ass."

He smiled, "What's the name of your ride?"

"I like to call my car Black Beauty. She can be sassy when she needs to be, believe me!"

We laughed in concert as we got into the car and began our mission.

"Black Beauty, huh?"

"What? You don't like the name?" I asked while staring ahead at the morning traffic.

"Okay, I will tell you what. I will change the name right now. What do you want to name my car?"

Carl smiled as he nodded and stared at the black leather bucket seats.

"How about Belinda the Beast?"

I laughed aloud. It was an unexpected name, but a welcomed one at that.

"Okay, I like it. Let's do it!"

"Really?" Carl was surprised at my sudden acceptance.

"Yeah, why not? Belinda the Beast, let's haul ass!" I declared while I accelerated down onto the freeway ramp. The traffic seemed light for an early Friday afternoon. The bridge overlooked the entire city. A cool breeze greeted us as we rolled down the windows.

"Do you like rock?" I asked.

"Yeah, I have a mixtape if you want to listen to it."

I curl my lip out in admiration. "Sure, put it in. Come on, let's jam."

I turned up the volume after hearing the guitar riffs and raspy singing.

"Yeah, I like this band. Is this ACDC?"

Carl nodded, "Yeah, Highway to Hell. Good song, right?"

"Not bad, I like it. Okay, let's talk about the mission. How should we do this?"

The engine growled loudly under the hood as I accelerated hard on the freeway.

"Here, exit here," he said while pointing at the upcoming exit sign. "Take two rights, then the taco stand will be over on Locust.

"All right, yeah, I have passed by here before."

The atmosphere felt more relaxed here since we were closer to the bay. The area has been known as the Millionaire's Club since only millionaires live in the high rises, which puncture the sky throughout the area, blocking the ocean's view. Several yachts and sailboats litter the ocean waters as we leaned against Belinda the Beast with our tacos.

"You asked me how we should do this, right?"

I nodded my head after stuffing my face with my shrimp taco. I was never a fan of seafood until I moved here. Now all I eat is seafood.

"My friend owns a bug exterminator store not too far from here. We could borrow his van, uniforms and show up."

After swallowing my delicious morsel, I nodded in agreement, "This is a good idea. I like this," I declared.

"Okay, let's finish up and head over there then. Michele owes me a favor anyway, so I might as well collect it."

"What's the name of your friend's store?"

Carl finished up his lunch and said, "Stop Bugging Me."

I laughed, "That's a good name!"

My partner smiled, "Yeah, I know, it was my idea!"

"Looks like my partner here comes up with some good names, too! I should give you a nickname."

He laughed and said, "I gladly accept whatever nickname you come up with, Hugh."

Chapter 4

Stop Bugging Me

"Hey Michele, how are you, man?" Carl asked as we stepped into the small store. The bell alerted the tall thin man standing behind the counter.

"Oh hey, what's up, Carl? Long time no see man, how are you? And who is your friend here?"

"Hi, I am Hugh Schpenus," I declared while shaking his hand. "Your accent, Russian?"

"Yeah, and you, Austrian?" he smiled.

"Yes, nice to meet you, Michele."

"You have an interesting name there, Mister Schpenus. You look like you can kick some ass, too. But listen, any friend of Carl is a friend of mine. So, what can I help you boys with?"

"Listen, Mich, we need your help. We're on an undercover mission to bust a local drug lord, and we need to borrow a van and some uniforms," asked Carl.

"Whoa, whoa, now come on, man, you know how I feel about things like this."

"I know, Mich, but listen, this guy right here, my partner, you don't want to upset him. I told him how great of a friend you are and how you owe me," my partner added tilting his head.

"All right, fine," Michele laughed nervously. "Anything for you, my friend. I have a uniform for you. But your big friend here, I don't know if I can find one in his size. It might be a little, you know," he paused while holding out his arms at his side. "A little tight."

"It's okay. I don't mind it being tight. Maybe it will stretch out."

Michele rubbed his spikey blonde head and said, "Just don't rip it, okay?"

After exiting from the closet with the uniform on, I could hear the threads reaching out in agony.

Carl and Michele looked at me and smiled.

"Looks good on you, right Michele?" Carl asked anxiously.

"Yeah, sure, whatever you say, man. Look, just don't rip it or else it'll cost you."

"You can bill the West End PD because they will pick up the tab."

"Oh, PD, huh? Listen, when you're done with this mission, I got some scumbags who owe me for some previous services and jobs. People you know, they never pay up around here."

"No deal," I declared coldly.

"All right man, no need to get your panties in a, what is it bundle? I don't know the American expression for this since I am still learning."

The white and gray van stood outside, parked beside Belinda the Beast. A sizable green insect, which resembled a fly, sat on the roof with the red logo on both sides. It was an obnoxious but marketable approach.

"I hope this plan of yours works," I said to Carl, who had on a red cap with the fly design and logo on the front.

"Don't worry, it will. We just have to play it cool."

As we sat in the van, the smell of chemicals and fumes lingered heavily in the air.

"What's the plan?" I asked while I rolled down the window.

"Okay, we'll show up and say someone called for an exterminator. I'll go in first, and you will follow close behind. We'll have the tanks on our backs and start sweeping the rooms. Look for anything suspicious that could help us nail this guy."

I curled my lip in recognition of this solid plan. "Not bad. I like this plan. Okay, what will our names be?"

"Good idea," added Carl. "We should give ourselves fake names. I will be Danny, and you can be Hans."

"Hans? That sounds like a guy who belongs in a symphony behind a cello."

Carl laughed and said, "Trust me, Schpenus, this will work."

"What's our signal to know when the job is done?" I asked while tucking my gun away in my boot.

"I will call you on the radio and say, no bugs found here."

"I got it, okay. Let's do this, partner," I said while holding up my fist.

Carl smiled and bumped my fist. "We got this, Hans," he reassured.

Chapter 5

Tina

The brakes squeaked loudly as the van pulled up to the intercom. In front of us was a large black gate. Through the bars, a large courtyard can be seen along with one large fountain. The place was heavily armed with guards and Dobermans.

"Hi, yeah, this is Danny from Stop Bugging Me. We received a call about some roach problem."

"Okay, roll up to the entrance," the deep voice said.

As the gates slowly opened, a weird sensation crossed my mind. This was my first assignment in what felt like a long time since I have had a terrific partner like Carl.

"Are you ready for this partner?" he asked after parking the van in front of the large mansion.

"Ready," I answered firmly.

After grabbing the large, heavy tanks, we made our way up the concrete steps when a scantily dressed woman opened one of the red double doors.

"Hi, are you, boys, from Stop Bugging Me?" she asked while staring at me.

"Yes," answered Carl. "Someone called about a roach problem?"

She patted her puffy curly blonde hair while keeping her eyes on me. "Funny, I don't remember anyone telling me about this phone call." She bent her knee forward while twirling her foot playfully in her red heel. "And what's your name, big boy? You sure are cute," she added while gently tapping her finger against my chest.

"Hans," I answered.

"Hans? Oh, where are you from? Your accent is sexy. Come on in, boys, my name is Tina."

Together the three of us entered the mansion. Inside, a large chandelier hung over the center of the room. Our footsteps echoed against the tiled floor and massive walls that displayed several portraits of Tina and Sanchez. There were also numerous paintings of random animals, including an elephant battling a rhino, two tigers pouncing on a gazelle, and a black panther roaring while climbing down a tree branch.

"Interesting décor," I declared while looking around the room.

"Oh, you like it?" Tina asked with a smile. "Maybe I should tell my husband to have one of you. You look cute in that uniform of yours, a real German schoolboy."

"Austrian," I added.

"What's that?" Tina snapped back.

"Uh, nothing, listen, where can we get started? Sorry these thanks are heavy," suggested Carl.

"Oh, yeah, sorry I got lost," she stated while winking at me."

"You can start here," she said while pointing at the windows, which were covered by the red velvet curtains.

"As for you, my lumberjack, you can follow me into the bedroom."

I turned and looked at Carl nervously.

"Uh, are you sure, miss? This is a pretty big room. It would be easier if my partner helped me here."

"Oh, I think you can handle it. I have a job for, what was your name again?"

"Schpenus," I accidentally blurted out.

Tina giggled like an immature cheerleader. "Hans Schpenus? Really? Oh, this will be fun and interesting. Come with me!" she declared while slapping my backside. "Oh wow, what a hard piece of meat you are packing!"

I smiled embarrassedly, and the two of us headed up the spiral stairwell.

Inside the bedroom, a king-sized bed covered in royal purple silk sheets sat at the center of the room. A large painting hung over the bed against the wall of two gray wolves staring mysteriously with their yellow eyes under a full moon.

"Interesting painting you have there," I stated nervously while looking at the painting.

"Listen, sweetheart, we don't have much time here. So, if you're going to do any inspections, I suggest you start here," she declared while jumping on the bed. Her tight light blue cocktail dress hugged her pale skin as she kicked off her red heels.

"All right," I added while placing the heavy tank on the floor. "I suppose I can start right here."

Tina giggled excitedly while wrapping her thin arms around my neck.

Then without warning, she ripped open the front of my uniform like a hungry beast. The white buttons scattered throughout the bedroom floor.

"Uh, are you sure this is a good idea?"

But before I could say more, our lips met and locked tight.

Chapter 6

Out of Time

Meanwhile, Carl quickly moved out of the living room and into the kitchen. Luckily, most of the

guards were outside patrolling the area. As he pretended to fumigate the room, he began opening and closing the drawers in hopes of finding evidence. Every drawer he pulled out contained no incriminating evidence.

"Hey, what are you doing here?"

The unexpected question from the guard startled Carl.

"Oh, sorry, sir, I was just checking your drawers."

"I can see that, and may I ask why?" he asked while holding up a submachine gun.

"Looking for any signs of roaches and rats," answered Carl.

"Whoa, wait, what? Did you say roaches? You better make sure you check every single area. Do you need me to send some men in here? If we see one, we can shoot it because we have plenty of bullets!"

Carl chuckled nervously and said, "No, that's quite all right. I suggest you clear the room, though. I don't want to hit you with any of this stuff." He held up the spray gun, "This stuff is extremely toxic. It was used in one of the wars."

"Oh yeah? I better get the hell out of here then. Listen, if you need anything, just holler. I suggest you hurry up though, the boss will be back in fifteen minutes. If he sees you in here with that thing, he'll want you exterminated," added the laughing guard as he walked out of the kitchen.

Carl turned and continued searching furiously throughout the kitchen. It was at that moment that he realized he missed one prominent spot beneath the kitchen sink. He quickly ran over and opened both doors. Inside, several chemical cleaning agents sat idle in front of a curved metal drainpipe. With his flashlight in hand, he laid on his back and aimed it upward, revealing a wrapped plastic grocery bag. He grabbed it with his hand and gently removed it from its tight hiding spot.

His eyes widened with excitement at what was found, a large stack of money and several incriminating photos of Sanchez making deals with unknown people, including an old woman wearing a headscarf. Behind him, the screen door leading to the garden opened abruptly. The door springs bounced and squeaked loudly, alerting him of the approaching guard.

As the guard entered the kitchen, Carl stuffed the bag into his uniform while closing the doors.

"Did you find anything you were looking for?" the guard suspiciously asked.

"Uh, no, nothing to report, sir. I did spray beneath the sink, though, just in case," he chuckled nervously.

"Hmm, okay," replied the guard as he pushed his sliding sunglasses up his nose. "I thought I heard the sound of a ruffling bag."

"Oh yeah, that was the spray. It makes that sound, and it's quite loud. As I said, it's dangerous stuff, so you may want to stay clear."

"Is that right? What was your name again?" the guard asked with an even more suspicious tone.

"Danny, my name is Danny. Nice to meet you. And you are?"

The guard ignored Carl's question and gripped his submachine gun tightly. At that moment, he noticed the strange bugle at the center of the exterminator's chest.

"What's that?" he asked while pointing his weapon at Carl's chest.

"Oh, this? It's nothing," Danny replied while he slowly brought the exterminator hose and gun closer to his leg.

"Hm, strange, doesn't look like nothing from this angle. Do me a favor, will you? Open up your jacket," ordered the man as he pointed his gun at Carl.

"Yeah, sure, no problem. Can I just set my zapper down?"

"Your what?" the guard asked while closely watching him as he slowly lowered the bug zapper gun.

"My zapper, see?" Carl said while spraying the guard's face with poisonous spray.

"Ah, what the hell, man! It burns! Ah! The sunglasses, they do nothing!"

Surprised by the guard's reaction, he wasted no time and quickly punched him in the face, instantly knocking him out. Knowing their cover was about to be blown, Carl decided it was time to leave.

He quickly ran up the stairs and could hear strange noises emulating from behind the closed bedroom door.

"Yeah, that's really nice!' Hugh's voice cried out from behind the door.

Forgetting his partner's cover name, Carl cried out, "Hugh, it's time to go!"

Suddenly a silence fell from behind the door. Then, the sound of a belt jingling signified whatever was transpiring from behind the door stopped. The door was violently pulled open, revealing a disheveled Tina and Hugh.

"Okay, time to go, huh?" I asked while attempting to button my shirt, forgetting I lost my buttons.

"What the hell happened to your uniform? Miche, er, the boss is going to be mad!"

"Oh, sorry about your uniform!" Tina declared from behind. "I can give you some money here," she said while stuffing several hundred-dollar bills into my back pocket. "Wait a minute, did he just call you Hugh? Is your name Hugh Schpenus? I thought it was Hans!"

"No, you're hearing things!" I said while the two of us hastily ran down the stairwell.

"Well, if your name is Hugh Schpenus, I must say the name fits you!" Tina shouted as she watched us leave from atop the stairwell.

Chapter 7

Headless Fly

After we loaded up the van and started it, my partner gave me an angry look.

"What the hell, man?"

"What?" I said, knowing exactly why he was upset. I left him alone, but it was against my will.

"You left me alone down there. I almost got killed, you know!"

"Sorry, I didn't want to blow our cover, especially since that was the boss' girl!"

"Yeah, okay, it's fine, you're right. If you didn't go with Tina, she would have made us leave, and I wouldn't have found this!" Carl said excitedly while pulling out a rolled sack inside a plastic bag.

"What is this?"

But before he could answer, gunfire erupted, shattering my window.

"That's them! That guy sprayed my eyes and apparently had his way with the boss' girl!" the guard yelled while rubbing his eyes.

More gunfire rang out, hitting the van, including the fly sitting atop of the fan. A shotgun broke through the air knocking off the insect's head.

"Oh shh, we better get the hell outta here!" Carl yelled while putting the van in gear and peeling away. The loud screeching tires cried out against the gunfire as bullets penetrated the vehicle's sides and back.

I pulled out my Beretta and returned fire. The guards jumped down and ducked as my shots missed them. As we drove down the path toward the exit, the front metal gates slowly opened while the guards continued firing at the van. The back windows shattered from their attacks causing us to lean our heads forward.

"Get down!" I yelled as we drove through the gates, which were still slowly opening. The van's sides became scratched and damaged, adding more insult to injury, primarily to our pride for not executing this operation more smoothly.

"I can't believe it!" Carl yelled while we drove away. "Are they following us?"

I turned around and could see the guards run out into the street, firing several more shots at us, but we were too far for the bullets to reach their target.

"No, it's clear!"

"Okay, good, but man, Michele is going to be pretty upset when he sees what happened to his van!"

"And his uniform," I added while touching the side of the buttonless shirt.

"Oh yeah, he's not going to be happy when he sees what happened to that uniform."

"But I didn't do it! I had that wild woman attacking me!" I yelled while removing the buttonless shirt from my body and tossing it at Michele.

"I don't care, man. You damaged company property."

Carl flashed a nervous smile and looked out the front door.

"What? What is it, man?" Michele anxiously questioned while streaking around the counter and running toward the front door of his store. "Oh my! No! What?" He began yelling words in Russian, which I assumed were words to express his anger. "What the hell, man? What did you do to my van? What happened to my van?" he knelt on the concrete sidewalk while crying out.

"Sorry, we ran into some pretty big bugs," I stated.

"What the hell kind of job was this?" he asked while touching the side of his van, which looked more like a giant dragon damaged it with its claws. "And my fly! What did you do to Vladimir? Why is his head missing?"

"He named his fly Vladimir?" I asked Carl while the two of us stood outside the entrance.

"Apparently so. Let's get out of here," my partner suggested.

"Okay but hold on." I approached Michele, "Here," I said while stuffing the money Tina gave me. "Take this. I hope it covers the damages."

As Michele surprisingly held the giant wad of cash, his eyes widened in amazement.

"Wow, man, where did you get this amount of cash? Okay! Yeah! This should cover everything and even get me another van! Maybe I can get Vladimir another girlfriend, but first, I need to fix his head!" He looked at us in shock, "Your friend here, I like him! You're all right in my book

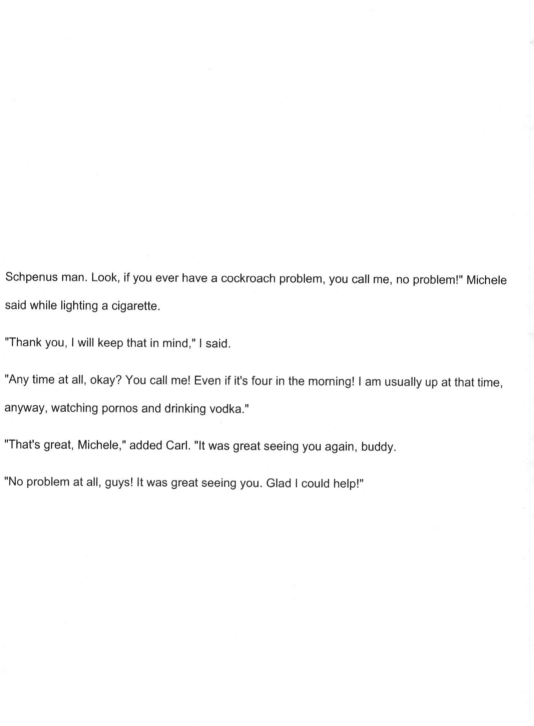

Schpenus man. Look, if you ever have a cockroach problem, you call me, no problem!" Michele said while lighting a cigarette.

"Thank you, I will keep that in mind," I said.

"Any time at all, okay? You call me! Even if it's four in the morning! I am usually up at that time, anyway, watching pornos and drinking vodka."

"That's great, Michele," added Carl. "It was great seeing you again, buddy.

"No problem at all, guys! It was great seeing you. Glad I could help!"

Chapter 8

Evidence

Back at the station, we sifted through the evidence. It consisted of twenty thousand in cash, passports containing Tina and Dirty Sanchez photos, and additional pictures with several deals with other crime bosses. One boss was dressed in what resembled a brown suit. The lettering on the back of the sign in the photo told me this was in Thailand.

"Wow," I said in shock. "I can't believe you stumbled upon this in the guy's kitchen! Why would he keep this stuff there out in the open?"

"Well, it wasn't really out in the open, you know. I had to dig deep for this, and it involved almost getting caught."

"Yeah, good point," I said.

"So, what should we do, partner?" Carl asked.

"I say we take this to Stacy right now. Let's go and get this guy!"

After hearing my statement, my partner slapped my hand excitedly.

"Boss!" I said as we entered his office.

"What is it? You two better have something good if you're bothering me. Don't you know it's my snack time?"

"Sorry, sir," said Carl. "But we have something here you may want to see," he tossed the bag onto Stacy's desk.

"What the hell is this?" he asked while opening up the bag. After what felt like hours of awkward silence, Stacy looked up at us. "Okay, look," he started while lighting a cigarette. "I am not going to ask you how because I don't want to know. But this is some good detective work. Whose idea was this?"

I opened my mouth to give Carl full credit when he declared, "It was a team effort, right partner?"

Noticing his wink, I looked at Stacy and smiled. "It was a joint effort, but mostly his idea. We had a little help, too."

"I said I didn't want to know the details! All right, this is good. Yeah, this is really good." He looked at us proudly as if he were a father and we were his sons. "When I worked the streets of Harlem and Detroit," he took a puff from his cigarette. "Never in a million years did I see such fine detective work like this! Well, other than what I used to do with my partner. And let me tell you both, I had a good partner. Glenn Parker. That guy was my most trusted friend. God bless his soul," he said while flicking ashes into the nearby ashtray.

"So, what happens now? Should we bust him now?"

Stacy shook his head at Carl's question. "No, no, they would be expecting us. Let's give him until tomorrow morning. You two go home and get some rest. Be back here at three in the morning." He looked at his silver watch, "This gives you about twelve hours until then, so go home."

After we returned to our desks, I looked over at my partner, who stared at me excitedly. "Can you believe it, man? We're going to take down one of the largest crime bosses!"

"Yes, but we must keep our cool. We go in there tomorrow, and we watch each other's backs, okay?"

"Of course, partner, you and me!"

"Listen, I have something that I want to give to you," I said while pulling out my gun from my desk drawer. "This is for you."

Carl was left speechless at the sight of the gun.

"This was the gun that I used during my first bust, and I want you to have it."

"Wow, thank you, Hugh! This is great!"

"Of course, but thank you for today, too. It was a great day."

Carl laughed aloud, "Of course, it was a great day. You met a woman."

I sat back in my chair and looked at my partner inquisitively.

"I don't get it," I said.

"What's that partner?"

"The woman back there, Tina, I don't understand what she meant when she said, 'I can see why your name is Hugh Schpenus,' I mean, this isn't the first time I'd heard this from a woman. I am just not sure what they mean by this."

Laughter erupted from my partner. "You're a riot, Hugh. I am glad we're partners. Listen, I am going to go home. See you back here."

Chapter 9

Back Home

I arrived home in my one bedroom. The evening sun was setting outside in the summer sky. Despite needing to sleep early, my body and brain were still too anxious about what transpired in just a few hours. Any case, big or small, always left me feeling this way. It was an uneasy feeling that I didn't care for.

My phone rang abruptly, "Hello?"

"Hi, Hugh, it's me," the woman stated sexily.

"Who is me?" I asked softly.

"Sharon, listen, what are you doing?"

"I have to sleep soon because I have a job to do tomorrow."

"A job?" Sharon wailed childishly.

"Come on, I miss you, Hugh, and that Schpenus of yours."

"I don't understand what you mean by that, Sharon. I have to sleep soon."

She breathed heavily into the phone, "I will tell you what, darling. I will come over and tuck you in."

"No, you won't. You will keep me up all night. How about after? Let's meet on Saturday. It's Friday, tomorrow's a school night."

She laughed at my reply.

"Fine, fine, we'll have it your way. You're such a tease, Hugh."

I smiled on the phone, still unaware of who I was talking to.

"I know, babe, tell you what, I will even buy you dinner."

"Oh, can we go to that restaurant again? You know it was so good!"

"Yeah, we can," I replied, still trying to remember who she was.

"Oh good I love the spaghetti from Mama Lucha's. What a great suggestion and night that was, huh?"

I laughed. Now I remembered who this was, sexy Sharon, as I liked to call her.

"That's right, Se, er, Sharon, it was a rather fine night."

After hanging up with Sharon, I began to pump some iron. I always like to lift a little before bed. I grabbed my one-hundred-and-fifty-pound hammer and started lifting under the moonlight. Sweat poured down my bulging muscles as I could feel the excellent pump. In my head, I envisioned the team moving in on the mansion tomorrow. There's Dirty Sanchez with his machine gun in hand firing at us, but Carl and I are there to save the day. This is a good daydream.

The scene changed to Carl and I standing at a podium in front of a large crowd. Beside us was the mayor giving us the key to the city. The reality of this is the fact that I never liked the mayor here. His name is Ronald Drummond, who has been rated as the worst mayor ever. He's one of the reasons why I have to work hard busting criminals around here.

After getting my workout in, my body felt exhausted and beat, so I made my way into bed and fell fast asleep.

Chapter 10

Unexpectedness

Carl sat in the car beside me as we arrived in front of the mansion. The rest of the team was nowhere to be found yet, which meant we arrived earlier than expected.

"What's the plan?" he asked me while loading his handgun.

"We go in guns blazing?" I suggested.

"I like it, let's do this! I will start firing first, then you'll come in from behind and unload some clips while I reload."

"Okay, I like this idea!" I replied.

Together we ran up the stairs leading up to the double red doors. Suddenly, Tina opened the doors unexpectedly wearing a white silk nightie.

"Hello there, I've been waiting for you!" she said as she wrapped her arms around me.

"Hi Tina, listen, I can't do this right now."

"Oh, you have time for one quick snack, don't you? I made your favorite," she said while suddenly lifting a tray containing a vast array of little wiener schnitzels.

"Come on, partner!" Carl yelled as he grabbed my arm, but the beautiful delicacies were too strong to pull me away from. I began eating them one by one. It was a unique and satisfying feast.

While I continued ignoring my partner, he was unexpectedly ambushed from behind by several guards.

"This is for spraying my face!" one of the guards yelled while dumping a bucket filled with starving piranhas on his face and body.

"Carl!" I cried out, but before I could help him, Tina grabbed my arm and shoved a giant stein filled with my favorite beer.

"Here, drink this big boy," she said while forcing the cool, crisp liquid down my throat.

It was an intoxicating fluid of joy and guilt. I wanted to help my friend, but this drink was too delicious to turn away from. After the contents of the golden beverage were empty, a loud belch erupted from my body. The most relaxing feeling ever escaped my body.

"Did you enjoy it?" Tina asked while staring at my satisfied grin.

"I did. Thank you, Tina," I replied.

"Good because now the trouble begins," she added.

"Trouble? What do you mean trouble?" I asked when suddenly my stomach began to churn and cramp strongly. With my body not hunching forward, I gripped my gut hard. "What is happening to me?" my voice cracked from the pain.

Tina laughed wickedly, "You just drank an entire beer and a bottle of anti-constipation medicine."

I lurched forward, and with my hands as my guide from falling forward, I walked farther into the mansion, passing a now possibly dead Carl. The henchmen pointed and laughed at my agonizing and uncomfortable pain. It was unbearable.

"Where is this giant Paul Bunyan giant lumberjack going?" Dirty Sanchez asked as he stood behind me beside Tina with his arm around her waist. "This should teach you to not sleep with my girl!"

"We..." I began to say, but the churning grew stronger.

"We what?" he asked while revealing a roll of toilet paper in his hand. "Tell me, Hugh, or else you will be in a deep mess," he chuckled manically.

"What do you mean?" I asked while I stood in front of the bathroom door. Another quake shook from within my stomach. "What did you do, Dirty Sanchez?"

He laughed aloud, "They don't call me Dirty Sanchez for nothing! Take a look inside. The bathroom."

I opened the door only to find an excellent and pristine toilet, but there was one problem, no toilet paper.

"No! What? How could you?"

He snickered devilishly while the rest of his crew continued laughing and pointing at my situation.

"You want this? It's so soft too, see?" he said while rubbing the roll against his face and mustache. "It's so soft, Schpenus, but you cannot have this!" Dirty Sanchez kicked me directly in my stomach without warning, knocking me back onto the bathroom floor.

The fall did not hurt as much as the kick, which resulted in an unwanted action. I could no longer sustain control over the pressure that was building within my bowels and stomach.

"No! It hurts!" I yelled while reaching out one last time for the toilet paper. "It hurts! Damn you, Dirty! I will get you for this!"

"You really think so, Schpenus? I'd like to see you try!" he laughed mockingly then closed the door locking me in.

I sat up and yelled, "No, Dirty Sanchez!"

Only to find myself sitting up in my bed. Sweat saturated my sheets as beads rolled down my back like rain on a window during a storm. I looked over at my clock, and it was two in the morning. It was time to go and get ready.

Chapter 11

Operation Dirty Takedown

Inside the armory, Stacy and the rest of the team stood together, looking over a large map.

"According to our detectives here," Stacy said while pointing at Carl and me. "This is where Dirty Sanchez lives. Our mission is to infiltrate his base. Now, he will be expecting us, so expect heavy resistance. Carl, I want you to take Schpenus and enter from the rear."

The team began snickering quietly.

"What is so funny? Do you think this is a joke? You think this is a game?" Stacy barked at us with a serious undertone.

"No, sir!" we answered in concert.

"Good, now listen up, people. I want this to go smoothly. No casualties. And no one, I mean no one, gets left behind! You got that?"

"Sir, yes sir!" we answered again in unison.

"Good, that's what I like to hear. Now let's move in two by two through the front entrance. Hugh Schpenus, you and Carl will go in from the rear and take out any resistance. I predict the bulk of the army will be covering the front."

"Are you ready, partner?" Carl asked while I holstered my handgun.

I smiled at him, "Yeah, we're going to take this scumbag down!"

"All right, ladies, let's move! It's go-time!" Stacy yelled out.

We all entered in single file into the police vans. The air outside was crisp for a moonlit summer night with puffy clouds hanging overhead. It felt like an October night with the tricks we'd brought to one of the biggest crime lords West End has ever seen.

"Sir," I said after we made our way toward the mansion.

"What's up, Schpenus?"

"How about a mixtape?" I suggested while handing over a cassette tape marked Hugh's Jams One.

Stacy grabbed it without further words and inserted it.

"I like this song," stated one of the nearby police officers.

"Yeah, this is a good one," added Carl.

"It sure is the final countdown. Dirty Sanchez is going to get what's coming to him!" I declared. Loud cheers followed my statement as we drove through the damaged gates.

"What the hell happened to the gates?" Stacy asked while we headed down the road toward the mansion.

"That would be us, sir," answered Carl.

"Good job, boys. I like it!" Stacy stated while flicking his cigarette through the open window.

Several guards noticed the van coming down the road and began yelling orders.

"All right, you two better get out here. We'll create a diversion," our boss ordered.

"You got it, sir!" we said in concert while jumping out of the slow-moving van.

Gunfire rattled as the van continued toward the front of the mansion.

"Looks like he's expecting us, huh partner?"

I looked at Carl and nodded in agreement, "Let's move."

We performed majestic rolls and dashes like two ninjas through the courtyard. The sound of running water from the large porcelain fountain concealed our footsteps. At the same time, we took advantage of the thick exotic purple rose bushes as cover. The sound of gunfire being exchanged like a savage currency reverberated loudly outside the front of the mansion. I could hear Stacy yelling several words laced deep with obscenities as he returned gunfire from his shotgun. It was a glorious moment that I wished to be a part of. But no, my mission lies elsewhere.

Together Carl and I reached our goal, the rear entrance of the mansion. Luckily only four guards stood in our way.

"What's the plan, partner?" Carl asked in a low whisper.

"Okay," I answered. "I will whistle the two guards over, and you can take out those two at the top of the stairs. Then I will meet you at the entranceway. Luckily, the sounds of gunfire from the front entrance should help us in case we use our guns, but let's try not to, okay?"

"Understood. Good luck, Schpenus!"

I nodded then whistled at the two guards while my partner quietly circled around the rosebush.

"Did you hear something?" asked the guard.

"Yeah, it sounded like a nighthawk."

"A nighthawk? What the hell is that?"

I whistled again, hoping this time it would draw the guards closer.

"There it is again; come on, let's check it out!"

Together the two guards dressed in black suits approached the rosebush I was hiding behind. I waited several moments, and then I attacked.

As I stood up, my presence startled them briefly.

"What the? Aren't you the Schpenus guy from earlier?"

"The name's Hugh Schpenus!" I declared while grabbing both of their heads and banging them together as if they were two watermelons.

Chapter 12

Kitchen Fun

With the two henchmen unconscious from my unexpected attack, I quickly stepped over them and ran up the stairs leading up to the back entrance of the mansion. My partner was busy fighting off both guards, and he was having trouble taking them both down from the looks of it.

"Hey, need a hand?" I asked while grabbing the shoulder of one of the guards.

"That would be great," he replied, only to suddenly realize I wasn't talking to him.

"Wait a second, you're the bug guys from earlier, I remember you!" the other guard said while pointing at Carl. "You're the jerk who shot that bug crap in my eye!"

"Oh, that was you?" Carl awkwardly answered. "Listen, I am sorry about that."

As the other guard threw a punch at me, I quickly blocked it with my arm and returned a right fist directly at his face. The impact pushed him back against the wall. To my surprise, he shook off my punch and came at me again, but this time he tried his luck with a front kick.

I quickly grabbed his leg, which left me with uncertainty on what to do next. As he tried to throw another punch, I beat him to it by performing a front kick of my own which landed directly in his crotch. It's a dirty move, but it gets the job done.

"Ah! That," he tried to complete this sentence while grabbing his nuts and berries.

"Hurt?" I answered before landing a right hook to his face.

I turned around and saw my partner standing over the guard he was fighting with.

"Everything okay?"

He exhaled heavily, "Yeah, let me collect myself for a moment. Why don't you go on ahead, okay? I'll catch up."

"Yeah, sure, I will meet you inside."

I kicked open the large wooden door and made my way into the dark kitchen. Numerous pots and pans hung over the stove. With the power being out, I found myself having trouble figuring out where to go next.

Another guard entered the kitchen from the front entrance and became startled from seeing my unexpected appearance.

"Who the hell are you?" he asked while fumbling around with his machine gun.

"I am your worst nightmare!" I answered while knocking the weapon out of his hands.

The guard stumbled back momentarily before grabbing a nearby kitchen knife. Like an angry wizard, he began waving it around at me, but before he could make any contact with my body, I grabbed one of the hanging frying pans. With the blade and pan making contact, we commenced a duel of the ages. He held a meat cleaver, and with both weapons in hand, I tried my best at reflecting both. Loud clings and clangs echoed within the kitchen, with the blades bouncing off the pan.

The guard, feeling frustrated, rushed in with the knife pointed at me while slashing the cleaver in a downward motion. With my attention focused on deflecting the weapon, the blade sliced into my shoulder.

"Argh!" I yelled while falling against a nearby cabinet.

"I got you now, Schpenus! You're mine!" the henchman declared as he rushed toward me for another attack.

A nearby flame caught my eye. I ignored the pain from the searing handle of the boiling pot of water and quickly removed it from the burning gas stove.

"Here, your soup is ready!" I yelled while tossing the hot boiling water onto the guard's face.

The pain sent him wailing in pain as he dropped his weapons and covered his face.

With my assailant unable to attack me, I threw two good punches at his face, which sent him flying across the room.

I exited the kitchen only to fend off two more guards. They have the advantage since they surprised me with their presence. One guard began throwing boxer punches while the other performed several karate kicks. It's tough to block against both of them, but I did my best to hold my own.

"Schpenus, get down!" Stacy ordered from afar while holding a large shotgun.

I jumped out of the way as he unloaded several shots, sending both guards through the flapping kitchen door, which thumped violently after they flew through it.

"You all right, pal?" he asked while helping me up.

"Yeah, no problem."

"Where's Carl?" Stacy followed up, noticing my missing partner.

"He's catching up. Where's Dirty Sanchez?"

"Upstairs with a hostage," he answered, exhaling heavily.

"Tina," I answered. My keen detective sense told me it had to be her. "He's holding her hostage. I will go and rescue Tina and defeat our enemy! Can you go and help Carl?"

Stacy smiled at me and nodded, "You got it, be careful, Schpenus."

"I will."

Chapter 13

Surprises

I ran up the spiral stairwell, and after reaching the top, the sound of a woman crying in distress greeted me. It was Tina. She was standing in front of me with Carlos Dirty Sanchez behind her.

"Well, well, well. You must be Hugh Schpenus. I heard you and my girl here had some fun earlier. He noticed the frying pan in my hand. He displayed his trademark laugh, which sounded like a mix between a bullfrog in heat and a broken ambulance siren. "What are you going to do with that? Cook me dinner? I would welcome that since Tina here never steps foot in the kitchen unless it's to eat my snacks!"

"I am sorry! I ate all of your chips!" she began wailing as he pressed the knife closer to her neck.

"Let's make this easy for the both of us, huh?" he said while eyeing the frying pan. "Drop the weapon."

"All right, I am putting it down," I stated as I slowly lowered the frying pan. My only chance now would be to hit Tina in the head lightly with it. This will most likely ruin any second chance with her, though.

As I lowered the frying pan, Sanchez smiled at me, which left me feeling reluctant and confused. But before I could figure out why, a gunshot rang out from behind, forcing me to completely drop the frying pan. As the bullet hit my arm, I turned only to see my partner, Carl, standing behind Stacy.

"Carl, what are you doing?" I asked while he pressed the revolver that I gave to him earlier against my boss' temple.

"I am fulfilling my end of the deal," he answered while looking at Sanchez.

I turned to look at the crime boss, who was smiling maniacally at us.

"They don't call me Dirty Sanchez for nothing now!" he laughed. "You see, your partner here is really my adopted son. I had him gain your trust Schpenus."

"How could you do this to me, Carl? I let you name my car! We shared tacos together!"

Carl smiled at me, "No hard feelings, but your car sucks, and Stacy," he said while looking down at the man's red sweater. "This is the ugliest red sweater I have ever seen. It makes you look like Bill Crosby's stunt double for a pudding commercial."

Carl's words suddenly sparked a flame within Stacy because, at that moment, my boss went berserk and showed total mayhem on the traitor. With one swift motion, Stacy drove his sharp elbow directly into my former partner's gut. The attack caused him to lose control of the revolver, and while this was unfolding, I jumped toward Tina and Sanchez.

Stacy drove a rear sidekick into Carl while grabbing the revolver and aiming it at Sanchez. As I tackled both Tina and Sanchez onto the floor, my hands knocked the small knife away from his hands. With the weapon clinging away like loose change, the tide turned to our advantage.

Sanchez looked up at me with amazement and said, "Now that was unexpected."

"Carlos Dirty Sanchez, you are under arrest," I declared as I placed and locked the handcuffs around his wrists.

"And what about your partner?" Stacy asked while pushing Carl down onto his knees beside Sanchez.

"You mean former partner? His days are done. And for the record, my car's name is Black Mamba!"

Stacy and I stood together as the two criminals were shoved into the back of a squad car, watching from a distance. Behind us, the sun slowly began to rise.

"Now I hope for the record you remember this," I stated while pointing at my boss.

A smile flashed across his face, "Come on now, I know what you're talking about. Your partner."

"Exactly, and this is why I work alone. No one can be trusted."

"Well, I have news for you buddy, I may have another partner for you."

"Oh great, and who might that be?"

"Me," Tina replied as she approached us.

"You? I don't understand."

Stacy laughed aloud while standing beside the young, scantily dressed woman.

"Tina here, or shall I say, Maggie, has been undercover for several months now. She's the reason why you were able to grab the knife so easily."

"During that tackle, I elbowed Sanchez right here where it hurts," she said while looking down below my waist.

I perk an eyebrow, "I see. Wait a minute, does that mean…"

"That's right," she replied while flashing a naughty smile. "You can say we went undercover together," Maggie winked as she strutted away.

"What did she mean by that Schpenus?" Stacy asked suspiciously.

I ignored his question and instead asked, "So, what's next, boss?"

"Oh, we're not done yet. We still have to take down the other crime bosses."

"No deal, I need a vacation after this."

Upon hearing my reply, Stacy bellowed a hearty laugh. "Don't worry, they will be waiting for you when you get back. And Schpenus," he said pointing.

With my arm around my new partner, I turned and looked at him.

"Try not to get shot again!"

"Oh, this?" I replied while holding up my bandaged arm. "It's just a flesh wound. I'll live."

"As long as the rest of you is intact, then we'll be just fine, right boss?" Maggie asked while winking at Stacy. Stacy laughed and walked away from us.

Hugh Schpenus and the Golden Dragon's Talon

Across the World Adventure Awaits

Chapter 1

The Thief

The helicopter flew low over the city. Neon signs danced along the busy Saturday night streets with the artificial lights blinking in deception like starlight. She looked down from the open helicopter door.

"There, right there, that's the one," she said pointing at a landing pad.

Under a moonless sky, the chopper landed on the roof of the tall building looking over Hong Kong. As the door opened, out stepped a woman dressed as a ninja. Only her eyes were visible under the dancing spotlights.

"Keep the engine hot. This won't take long," the woman ordered the pilot.

Quickly and quietly, the woman scurried along the roof under the dark night sky. She wrapped her fingers around the ventilation grate and gently yanked it toward her thin body with her gloved hands. Thanks to the chopper's whirling blades, the sounds from the clanging metal went unnoticed inside. She affixed a grappling hook onto the side of the vent, then released a long black rope down the shaft. Like an uncoiling viper, it stretched out until it disappeared into the darkness below.

She took hold of the rope and then vanished into the ventilation shaft.

"I am inside," she whispered through her commlink.

"Good, make sure you retrieve the item without being detected," the deep-voiced man said on the other end.

"Don't worry, Phucc. I will."

"Good," Phucc replied.

Like a panther slowly prowling through a tree, the thief crawled through the ventilation system until finally reaching her target. Through the grated vent, a light shined over a tall glass case. Inside, a small golden claw rested still. At the end of the claw, there were various colored gems affixed to each talon. She has successfully reached her destination.

"I have found the target," she whispered.

"Excellent, I will delay the cameras on my end," Phucc responded.

CCTV cameras slowly moved side to side below, monitoring the entire room within the art gallery. The suspecting guards sat in the large room staring at the monitors while still oblivious to the thief's presence thanks to the disruption showing no unwanted guests. The woman quietly loosened and removed the vent, then she slithered down onto the museum floor. The display of the dragon's talon greeted her beneath the spotlight. The glimmer from green, blue, purple, red, and yellow gemstones filled her eyes as she slowly made an incision within the glass. It was a perfect circle.

She carefully touched the artifact and, with little effort, removed it from the display case. With little time to admire the beautiful piece, the woman swiftly placed the talon in her knapsack. The woman placed a polaroid photograph of Hugh Schpenus and a note in place of the now-removed item.

Then in one swift motion, the thief jumped up into the vent and made her way back to the rooftop. The helicopter sat with its giant rotor spinning, waiting for her return.

"Do you have it?" asked the pilot.

The woman nodded and entered the chopper.

"I do. Let's return to Bangkok," she replied while buckling herself in.

Chapter 2

Baseball

"I still don't understand. The guy is called a shortstop, but he's not actually short. Why is he called this?"

Stacy shook his head while flagging the Beerman, "Because he's supposed to stop the guy short."

I laughed, "If he is supposed to stop the guy short, why not just put two guys there then? Call one the shortstop and the other the longstop. And what is the deal with this mascot? It's a monk?"

"Look, man, this is supposed to be a fun company outing. Why are you asking so many damn questions? Don't you have baseball games like this in Austria?" Stacy grabbed two beers and handed one to me. "Here, just get drunk and enjoy the game."

"Oh good, thank you. Yeah, this game would be pretty boring without this beer," I added while chugging some of the cold beer, which was too watery for my taste. "They put more ice than beer in this."

Just then, the player cracked his bat against the ball, causing the crowd to stand up.

"What's going on? Why are we standing up? This is like being in a church!"

Ignoring my remark, Stacy began to cheer loudly, "Hell yeah! He hit a grand slam! Yes!"

"Cool, isn't there a pancake breakfast thing called this at some diner?"

Stacy shook his head and laughed, "I can't take you anywhere, can I?"

I looked at my boss and smirked, "I know one place where we can go, but I won't behave much."

My boss laughed as we sat down. Sweat rolled down our foreheads under the July summer sun.

"I am not going with you to some strip joint," he remarked.

"Why not? It's a fun place. You will like it!"

"Man, I got a wife and two kids. How is seeing a pair of breasts going to help me? And I have to pay to see them. I can see that at home for free."

I laughed and replied, "It's about the experience."

"The experience? If you want an experience, you need to find a woman to settle down with. That's what you need," declared Stacy.

I smiled at him and replied, "The day I find a wife is the day hell will freeze over."

"Excuse me," the man wearing a suit called out from a few seats down. "I am looking for a Hugh Schpenus."

Several fellow officers dressed in civilian clothing erupted in laughter at the man's question.

"I am Hugh Schpenus. What is going on?" I announced hastily.

"Hugh? You need to come with me right now. This is an international matter."

Stacy and I stood up in unison and together we made our way toward the man.

"Excuse me," he said rudely while placing his hand on Stacy's chest. "I only need Schpenus."

The remark caused my captain to shove the guy back, nearly knocking him down onto the concrete stairs.

"Don't you ever touch me! Don't you know who I am? I am Stacy Jackson, and I will kick your ass!"

"Listen, whoever you and whatever your name is," I interjected. "He needs to come with me because he is my boss and needs to be involved."

The man collected himself and said nothing further as the three of us exited the stadium.

Chapter 3

Dragon's Fire

She cupped the golden Dragon Talon in her hands. The golden scales shimmered brightly as the gemstones at the end where the actual talons were sparkled and twinkled like extraterrestrial starlight.

"Exquisite piece, isn't it?" Phucc questioned while smiling gleefully at the magnificent piece. His toupee covered most of his fifty-six-year-old head, but his age was starting to show within his facial features and expressions. His eyes showed more wrinkles when he'd smile. Sitting in the wooden chair behind his cherry oak desk, he leaned forward in his caramel-colored brown suit.

Born to a Thai mother and Chinese father, Phucc Yue moved to Thailand after spending the first half of his life in Hong Kong.

"It is beautiful, sir, but why did you request that I leave that photo behind?"

He leaned forward and flashed a smile filled with crooked and yellow stained teeth.

"I thought you would never ask Pornthip."

Pornthip gently placed the piece on Phucc's desk and slowly stepped away. Her long black hair shimmered under the dimly lit office that was looking over Siam Square. Below the hustle and bustle of the denizens moved about this late July night. She was tall for a Thai woman, but her thin physique was never underestimated because she was a trained fighter and assassin, Phucc's most loyal partner. She stood straight in front of her boss with her arms behind her back. Her black tight leather outfit revealed her beautiful body.

"You see, that photo of the man you left at the scene of the crime is the bane of my existence," he said while slamming fist onto the top of his desk.

"This bastard costed me millions a year ago when he took down Carlos Dirty Sanchez. And now," he clasped his black leather gloves together. "Consider that photo as a calling card. Hugh Schpenus will come to Thailand, and when he does, we will be waiting for him."

Phucc turned his chair around to face the large office windows. The neon psychedelic lights danced playfully against the window and his eyes.

Chapter 4

Thailand

"Where am I going?" I asked in shock.

"I said Thailand. There you will make contact with one of our agents. His name is Michael Cleveland."

"How do I know what he looks like?" I asked the suited man sitting behind the desk in the interrogation room. "And why are we here? I told you I had nothing to do with that missing bird claw."

"Dragon's Talon," the man answered crassly.

"Whatever it is, look, I have never been to Thailand, and I am not too comfortable flying that far from here."

The agent leaned forward and ran his fingers through his black slicked-back hair. "Look, Schpenus, I get it. But right now, you're the main suspect in this case. You may not have physically been there to steal this antiquity. Still, the Thai government considers you a suspect despite your involvement."

"That's the thing!" I said in vexation. My thick Austrian accent echoed inside the room. "I was never involved! Do we even know who is really behind this?"

The agent sighed out of his own frustration, "No, we don't."

The door opened abruptly, breaking the conversation. Stacy and another agent entered the room.

"Hey Hugh," Stacy calmly greeted me. It was great to have him here since he was my close friend and colleague. The tension in the room eased a bit as he smiled at me and nodded. "The FBI has filled me in on what's going on. Listen," he said, placing his hand on my shoulder. "You take all the time you need out there. You're going to love it out there, buddy," he added with a grin. "You're going to love Thailand. The food, the nightlife, it's right up your alley."

"No deal," I replied coldly as I stood up.

The agent stood up in concert and held out his arm, stopping me from leaving the room. "Schpenus, you really don't have a choice in the matter. Either you go to Thailand to clear your name, or you'll end up in prison for a crime you say you didn't commit. The choice is yours."

"Can you at least tell me what this thing is that I am being accused of stealing?"

"The Golden Dragon's Talon," he answered sternly. "It's a priceless artifact dating back to the Ming Dynasty. It was on display at the museum in Bangkok until the end of the year."

"So, it's priceless. Okay, whoever stole this, do you think the thieves will try to sell it?"

"No, Hugh," replied Stacy. "There's more to this."

"Oh? And what's that?" I asked while looking over at my boss, who was still dressed in his white and blue jersey from the baseball game.

"There is a rumor that inside this claw thing is a paper containing America's secret launch codes."

"What?" I was astonished. "How the hell was that in there?"

The agent interrupted, "We do not know, but you must retrieve this. Only you can penetrate deep enough into this mission. Whoever is behind this apparently is targeting you, so give them what they want, Hugh Schpenus."

"All right, I will do it. I will go to Thailand and find out who is behind this!" I replied sternly.

"Good," replied the agent. "It's not like you really had a choice," he added while chuckling. "You will find Cleveland running one of the local clubs. It's called Twisted Kitties. It's not far from your hotel."

"What does he look like?" I asked while putting on my black leather jacket.

"Oh, you won't miss him," added Stacy. "He looks like me, except he has a big afro."

Chapter 5

The Land of Smiles

The short, tanned man eyed me suspiciously, "Where you going?" he asked with a broken English accent.

"I need to go to Twisted Kitties," I replied while opening the door of the green taxi cab.

"Oh, you go for fun time. You just arrive, too!" the man laughed aloud as he hopped into the driver's seat.

I tossed my small brown duffle bag into the back seat and sat down. The loud leather rubbed against my blue buttoned-down sweaty shirt, emulating a sound of flatulence. This unexpected and accidental sound caught the driver's attention causing him to shake his head in disgust. I could feel the humidity seeping in through the opened windows. I was not prepared, nor did I expect such sweltering heat. This was both unbearable and nothing like West End.

"Where are you from?" the driver asked curiously while navigating the small Toyota through traffic.

"I am from a city in America called West End."

"Eh? South Bend? I have never been there, Indiana, right? My brother's wife's sister's friend's mother's son lives there. He said, very cold there."

I wanted to correct him but decided I wasn't really in the mood for small talk after sitting on a combination of layovers and flying for over eighteen hours.

As the cab continued toward its destination, the setting sun over the horizon caught my eye. It was a beautiful scene as the car crossed a beautiful white suspension bridge. The long beams reminded me of the Golden Gate, but this one stood out against the yellow and red sky.

"First time here?" the driver asked while noticing my gaze of amazement as I continued staring at the skyline and sunset backdrop.

"Yeah, it is," I replied.

A sea of people consisting of both tourists and locals flooded the streets. I could see several restaurants and businesses with their flashing, fluorescent, neon lights in every direction. A neon sign of a dancing gold dragon reminded me of why I was here. It was not for pleasure, but for business. I needed to clear my name and find out who was behind this.

"This city is quite beautiful, but mysterious," I remarked.

"Oh, yeah, I love it here. I was born in Phuket. Are you traveling in BKK only?"

"Yeah," I answered the driver while locking eyes with a beautiful Thai woman who was walking down the street beside the car. She flashed a flirtatious smile at me.

"Oh yeah, pretty girl," said the driver as he waved at the young woman who embarrassingly looked away. "Thailand, the land of smiles. You farang come here to steal our women," he sarcastically said while laughing. "You go to Twisted Kitties to steal one, eh?"

"I am meeting a friend," I responded.

"Oh, friend, right, mmhmm," the driver commented while chuckling.

Moments later, the cab arrived at Twisted Kitties.

Chapter 6

Twisted Kitties

The air outside was humid and sticky. It was unbearable for me due to my demanding size and physique. Beads of sweat rolled down both my face and muscular body, which was saturated against my brand new thin blue shirt. I brought along my "cruise wear" for this trip in hopes that it would be sufficient and light enough to withstand the rumored heat. Still, after spending just fifteen minutes standing outside the entrance, I was ready for a new shirt.

A trilby sat at the top of my head while thin white pants and brown loafers adorned the rest of my body. From the looks I was receiving from the foot traffic, I looked more like a retired Florida local than a Thai tourist, especially since my towering presence caused me to stand out like a rotten orange in a basket of fruit.

"You come in here," the woman in the red cocktail dress said while gently grabbing my wrist. Despite her petite size, she demonstrated an unexpected strength.

"Yeah," I replied. "I am looking for my friend, Michael Cleveland."

The woman remained silent while pulling me further inside the club. Loud new wave and electronic dance music filled the air as we weaved through the crowd. I waved my arm in hopes of keeping the thick heavy cloud of cigarette smoke away from my face. Flashing lights and lasers bounced in every direction giving me an unwanted headache.

"You sit here," the woman ordered as she pointed at a lone table near the bar.

After sitting down, the woman disappeared into the crowd, leaving me alone and feeling bewildered. This is not what I expected the first moments would be like in this foreign and unfamiliar place. I looked around and noticed the majority of the people inside were locals, with a few foreigners sprinkled in.

"What do you drink?" the woman returned while placing a small square napkin on the small round table.

"I am looking for someone," I replied.

"What? You drink beer? Okay," she answered while she turned and walked away from the table.

I shook my head annoyed while holding up my arms in frustration. "Does anyone speak English around here?"

"I do," the unexpected voice answered. "First time here?" the man asked as he pulled up a chair to my table.

I smiled while exhaling a sigh of relief at the sight of another foreigner, who resembled the description of my contact given by Stacy.

He wore a tight green t-shirt containing a beer logo with two elephants on the front and blue jeans. From his muscular build, I could see this guy could hold his own in a fight.

"Nice to meet you. I am Hugh, Hugh Schpenus."

Upon hearing my name, the man smiled and chuckled lightly. "You're Hugh Schpenus? I was expecting you. My name is Michael Cleveland, but most people just call me Cleveland. You look like you could take on an army!"

Before I could respond, the waitress returned with my beer and greeted Cleveland.

"Is he with you?" she asked her boss.

"Yeah, he is, don't worry about a thing, buddy. I will take care of you. Have you been to your hotel room yet?" Cleveland asked while observing me drinking my beer.

"No, I haven't, not yet. Oh man, I left my bag in the cab!" I declared while realizing my bag was missing. "I got distracted by a woman," I added.

Cleveland laughed and said, "Don't worry about it. That happened to me too when I first stepped foot in this country. We'll get you some new swag."

"Thanks, good thing I have my passport and wallet in my pocket, or I would have really been screwed. That was my cruise wear, though."

"Cruise what? You can't be dressed like that here in BKK. You'll stand out like a giant tree, even though you're as tall as one here. As it is," he said while eyeing my muscles protruding against my blue cruise wear shirt. "You look like you belong in a damn ring. Have you ever considered fighting?"

"What do you mean? I don't understand."

Cleveland laughed and slapped me on the shoulder, "Don't worry about it, man, listen. You must be tired. Meet me back here tomorrow. I will take you out for some lunch, and we'll hit up a spa. Then we'll talk shop. I will have some new swag sent to your room upstairs, a private suite," he added with a wink.

"Okay, thank you, Cleveland."

The man shook his head, "Don't mention it. I am here to help you. After all, I know you're innocent!"

Surprised by the man's remark, I sat forward while clutching my drink, "You do?"

"Of course! And I have a feeling I know who is behind all of this!"

"You do?" I gasped.

"Yeah, listen, for now, relax. Eat some food. I recommend the Kow Pad."

"I am not in the mood for beef. How about just some fried rice or something?"

My question caused Cleveland to erupt in heavy laughter.

"Kow pad is fried rice. Man, you have a lot to learn!"

Chapter 7

Steamer

"So, what did you think of the food from lunch?" Cleveland asked as we entered the small building, resembling someone's house rather than a legitimate business venue.

"It was interesting looking, but I liked it. I never had a whole fish like that. It was so fresh, too."

He nodded and replied, "Yeah, you get some good food out here. I could never go back to West End."

"Oh, you are from there?" I asked in a surprised tone.

"Yeah, a long time ago. I used to be Stacy's partner. Did he ever mention that?"

"He did say he had a partner in Detroit and Harlem, but never in West End."

After entering the steam room, the two of us, now dressed in towels, sat alone on bamboo benches while a large cloud of steam filled the room.

"Yeah, I figured he didn't mention me. He wasn't my partner but my mentor. We didn't really see eye to eye, you know what I mean?" Cleveland said while picking at his teeth with a thin toothpick.

"I understand. Stacy can be a little difficult and rough around the edges."

"You're telling me, but listen," he said with a serious look. "That man will take a bullet for anyone, no questions asked. He's the best man. And any friend of his is a friend of mine."

As we shook hands, I nodded in satisfaction, "You're a pretty cool dude Cleveland."

"Thanks, man, you too. Where are you from originally? I noticed your accent, Austria?"

"Yeah, I was born in a small town there, Bad Ischl."

"Bad ish, huh?" Cleveland replied. "Never heard of it, but I will tell you two things. One, BKK is no bad ish, but I know West End can be."

"It has its rough areas, I agree, but I like it there. The coast is beautiful," I added.

Disregarding my comment, Cleveland continued, "Two, I heard what you did out there last year. Taking down Dirty Sanchez. That was some real dangerous ish right there."

"Yeah, I lost a partner during that mission," I commented.

"I heard about that. I wasn't going to say anything about this, but just know that I am sorry about what happened. Sucks, but hey, I am not a traitor, and I will never be. Now, if you'll excuse me, I gotta drain the main vein," Cleveland remarked while he stood up and left me alone in the steam room.

I sighed and thought about my former partner Carl. The last time I gelled with someone like this was with Carl, who turned out to be a traitor secretly working for Dirty Sanchez. After the two of us went undercover and took down the crime lord, my former partner double-crossed me and threatened to take my life. The last thing I heard about my former partner, Carl, was that he was killed in prison.

After sitting alone for what felt like over twenty minutes, I began to wonder what was taking Cleveland so long. Feeling concerned for my new friend, I exited the steam room only to find several clothed men standing outside waiting for me. In front of the wooden door, I found myself alone in the men's dressing room with five men who looked tough and ready to fight.

At this moment a part of me wondered if Cleveland betrayed me after all, I sighed and readied myself for a fight.

"Listen, I don't know what's going on, but tell Cleveland he is a jerk for double-crossing me."

The men ignored my remark and moved in. I stepped forward and threw the first punch, immediately knocking the first guy out. The second and third gentlemen attacked in unison. The second man threw a punch, but I deflected it gracefully, but this caused me to lose my footing in the process. As I fell forward into a nearby locker, the third man kicked my stomach. Then the fourth man threw a punch, which landed directly at the side of my head. Unprepared for both the attack and the unexpected power from it, I found myself falling face-first onto the tile floor.

Chapter 8

Captured!

The cold water splashed against my face harder than going down a toilet bowl-shaped waterslide.

"Argh, what the hell? Where am I?" I yelled angrily.

"You are safe for now, in my meeting room," the spiffy-dressed man answered.

I quickly surveyed the room when I realized where I was: Tied up and bound to a small wooden chair. Overhead a bright light dangled freely. The heat from the exposed lightbulb added to the awkwardness I was feeling from being in what this man considered a "meeting" room. The gray concrete walls and floor reminded me of a place that I was trapped in a long time ago. That was a part of my past that I would hope to never relive.

"Who are you?" I asked impatiently. "What am I doing here? Where is Cleveland? I want to talk to that traitor!"

The man chuckled and replied, "I would ask you the same thing. It seems your friend has gone missing. But lucky for you, we have you as bait."

"Bait? I am not a fish!"

"Quiet!" the man snapped harshly. "Now, let me tell you who I am and why you are here," he said calmly while signaling one of his henchmen over. After whispering something cryptic into the young man's ear, the man turned and smiled at me. "I know who you are, Hugh Schpenus."

"That's great, but who are you?"

He chuckled at my question, "Phucc Yue."

"What did you say to me?"

"Phucc Yue," he replied calmly.

"Do you kiss your mother with that mouth?"

"No, you idiot! That is my name, Phucc Yue! It's Puck-Yu! Enough of this! This isn't a game!" he yelled frustrated. "I want you to meet the one who will be ending your life now, Pornthip. Say hello to Hugh Schpenus."

"Wow, talk about an interesting name," I crassly remarked.

"Shut up!" the young woman yelled while slapping across my face like a rabid sloth.

I licked my inner cheek and could taste a hint of blood. The metallic liquid tickled my taste buds. "That was not very nice."

"See you, Mister Schpenus," Phucc said as a smile crossed his face. "Pornthip, please take care of this gentleman, but try not to be too rough."

"Wait, come back here! Tell me what I am doing here!" I demanded angrily.

"Oh, you will find out soon enough," added the man as he entered the elevator.

Pornthip signaled one of the two henchmen, then she looked over at me. "Nice to meet you, Hugh Schpenus. I am Pornthip."

The man returned, pushing a cart containing several surgical and dental tools that rattled loudly as the metal cart vibrated against the concrete floor. She admired the surgical instruments as the henchman rolled it beside her. She gently picked up a dental pick while whipping her long black ponytail behind her shoulder.

"Leave us," she sternly ordered the other two guards, who, without question, abided and left the room through the stairwell.

She slowly approached me while holding the dental pick in her gloved hands. Her black leather boots tapped heavily against the floor.

"What do you plan on doing with that?" I asked her calmly while devising a plan to get out of the situation.

"Do you know why we brought you here?" the young woman nonchalantly asked while smiling at me seductively. Her red lipstick revealed a pearly white cavern. Her pale face made me wonder if she was a vampire.

"I don't know, to show me a good time?"

She chuckled softly, "Funny. You made my boss lose a lot of money last year. Do you know what you've done?"

"Last year in 1985? Yeah, I did a lot of things lady, how about refreshing my memory?" I sarcastically answered.

"Does the name Dirty Sanchez mean anything to you?" she asked while leaning in and breathing sensually onto the side of my face and neck.

"Yeah, it rings a bell," I answered as I felt goosebumps slowly rise through my neck and arms. A shiver ran through my body causing me to jerk slightly.

"You costed my boss a lot of money when you took Dirty Sanchez down. And for that," she calmly said while standing over me examining the dental pick. "You must pay."

"Wait a minute, what if I told you I have hidden Dirty Sanchez's money, and I am willing to strike a bargain."

"I would say you're lying, but I will play along," she replied while flashing a provocative smile.

"Come here, honey, lean in, and I will tell you where it is. I don't want to say it too loud in case anyone is listening," I said in a low voice.

As Pornthip leaned in, I decided it was time to execute my only idea from this makeshift two-minute plan that I made. With one quick and effortless move, I headbutted her directly into her face. The impact knocked the young woman onto her backside. Shocked by the sudden attack, the woman stood up and ran toward me out of anger, but I was prepared for this reaction.

Using my body weight, I forced the chair back, causing it to fall backward onto the floor. The impact from my body caused the wooden chair to break. With my feet now free, I kicked Pornthip's knee, knocking her face-first onto the floor.

With the woman in close distance to my brown suede loafer, I gave her a quick and effective front kick directly aimed at her forehead. The move knocked her out instantly. I flipped forward, landing gracefully onto my feet. Since my hands were still bound, I ran up to the cart and turned around to grab a scalpel.

It took some effort and patience, but after a short moment, I was finally able to cut myself free. Now it was time to confront her boss.

Chapter 9

Confrontation

I stepped inside the elevator while carrying the unconscious woman. The last thing I wanted to do was leave her down here with all of the weapons and possibly have her escape, too. A song that resembled a cross between Twinkle Twinkle Little Star and Fur Elise played through the static ceiling speaker within the elevator. Phucc turned around in his office chair as he sat behind his desk and smiled as the elevator doors slowly opened. But that smile slowly faded as he saw me standing there with his most loyal assassin unconscious and dangling over my shoulder like a lifeless doll.

"Hi, your girlfriend just couldn't handle what I had to offer her," I said sarcastically while tossing her body onto the red-carpeted floor.

This unexpected event caused Phucc Yue to stand up in anger and disbelief. How did this man beat his most skilled assassin, unless Schpenus was a man he shouldn't have underestimated?

"It seems I underestimated you, Mister Schpenus. You are a lot harder to beat than I thought."

"Phucc Yue, did you really think I would go down so easily?"

The crime boss pressed a secret red button beneath the top of his desk. Behind him, the night sky and glow from the city below painted the background like a classic martial arts movie. Phucc Yue slowly moved around the desk while keeping his eyes focused on me. I was unaware that this scumbag just triggered a secret alarm. Deciding he needed to buy time before his henchmen showed up, Phucc Yue began stalling.

"You farang are all the same. You come here thinking you can do whatever you want," Phucc declared while cracking his knuckles through his black leather gloves. "I think it's time I teach you some manners!"

"I am not a fang or whatever that is. I am Hugh Schpenus and I am all ready for you, teacher."

As Yue positioned himself to attack, Pornthip suddenly jumped onto my back wrapping her arms around my neck. The surprise move caused me to awkwardly stagger forward with the woman riding on my back like a donkey rodeo.

"I will kill you, you stupid Schpenus!" she yelled while attempting to put me in a sleeper hold.

Phucc laughed happily upon seeing his assassin's surprise attack and decided it was time for him to make his escape.

"See you later, Mister Schpenus!"

I wanted to respond, but the woman's hold was starting to cause me to slowly lose consciousness. I began moving my body around in a circle, hoping this would flick the woman off of me, but no, she held on tightly like an anaconda. Noticing a large mirror, I quickly ran toward it, then turned, and with her back facing the mirror, I jumped back directly into it.

A loud crash caught Phucc's attention as he was exiting the room.

"No! Pornthip!" he cried out as she fell lifelessly onto the red carpet. Large icicle-shaped shards of glass stuck out of her back as if she were a porcupine.

"You killed her! No!" he yelled while charging at me like a ravenous zombie.

"Crime doesn't pay!" I responded as the two of us clashed like two titans.

Phucc threw the first punch, which impacted the side of my face while I threw an uppercut directly at his chin. The hit caused me to lose my footing momentarily. My attack caused Phucc to fly across the room onto a wooden coffee table, which broke instantly.

As we both recovered, the reflective elevator doors opened in the distance. Phucc stood up with a smile, assuming his guards were finally going to show up. But, to his disappointment, it was Cleveland and several Thai police officers.

"Hey, pal, sorry I am a little late but fear not, Cleveland has arrived!"

I was stunned to see the man I wrongfully accused of being a traitor. I was speechless.

"Look out behind you, man!" Cleveland yelled as Phucc charged at me with a knife.

As I turned around, my reflexes blocked the knife attack with my arm as I screamed, "Phucc Yue! I don't think so!" Then, in one swift motion, I threw another punch at his face, sending him flying back onto the floor.

Cleveland laughed proudly and ordered the men to take Phucc and the woman, who was somehow still alive, into custody.

"Cleveland, what the hell! Where did you go? I waited for you."

"Oh, yeah, about that man, I am sorry. I got a little tied up," he answered sarcastically.

"I have to tell you something, I thought you were," but before I could finish my sentence, Cleveland interrupted, "I know, man, I get it. You thought I was a traitor."

Feeling remorse for the false accusation, I held out my hand and said, "I am sorry. I hope we can still be friends."

Hearing my words brought a smile to Cleveland's face. "Friends? No way, man, we're brothers!"

"You son of a bitch!" I declared as our hands locked. "You had me going there for a second!"

Cleveland laughed, "Consider that payback! So, what happens now, my brother? Are you going to stick around here for a bit? BKK could use a man of your size Schpenus."

The man's kind offer sounded enticing, but I firmly held out my arm and kindly rejected the offer. "As much as I love the food, the women, and even you, my brother, I must decline. My place is back home. Plus, who is going to watch Stacy's back? You know…"

"I get it, man, I get it. I will tell you what. When the time is right, know you are more than welcome to come back. Mi casa es su casa!"

I laughed and replied, "Likewise! If you're ever in West End, look me up! I am sure Stacy would be happy to see you, too!"

Chapter 10

Vacation

"Schpenus, I am impressed! You handled yourself well out there. You took down another crime boss, recovered the artifact and the codes, and I hear Cleveland offered you a job, too!"

I laughed and confidently replied, "Stacy, you know my place is here. Plus, who is going to watch your back?"

Stacy chuckled as he sat at his desk, "Well, it's a good thing you're back because I have another job for you. Did you know there's another crime boss who's angry at you? Oh, but you're not going to like this one. She lives in Russia. And you know winter is coming!"

I waved my hand disregarding what my boss had implied. "Forget it. I need a vacation."

"A vacation? You? Where in the hell are you going?" he asked, lighting a cigar.

I turned around, approached my boss, and snatched the cigar away from his mouth.

"Hey, that was my last one!" Stacy exclaimed while I took a puff and smiled.

"Boss, don't you know smoking is bad for your health? I am already saving your life, see?" As I turned to leave his office, Stacy laughed and replied, "Fine, fine, but when you get back, we will talk!"

Hugh Schpenus and the Bad Babushka

It is time to go out with a bang!

Chapter 1

Russia

"Mama," the man said nervously to the elderly woman who was simply known in the criminal underworld as Mama. She sat on the luxurious red velvet couch. Behind her, the crackling flames within the fireplace danced.

"What is it?" Mama replied as she sat forward. She wore a violet wool sweater, a red headscarf, and a dress with tan stockings while flashing a smile of stained yellow teeth. "He is dead. You are the only one left now."

She pushed the leaning black-suited man away from her while leaning forward over the glass table. A tiny fresh teacup of Earl Grey steeped in front of her. The wind and snow outside reminded her of the dreary December night. Winters in this part of Russia were difficult for the uninitiated.

After taking a sip from her porcelain cup of tea, she lowered the cup, causing a gentle clang. The sound caught the suited man's attention. He wanted to console her but, instead, decided to keep his distance. The man he was referring to was a past lover of hers. Mama had many lovers, but this man was special to her.

"Phucc Yue," she said his name with a heavy sadness.

"I am sorry, Mama," replied the man.

"Who? Who did it? Tell me Jenya," Mama snarled back. She was an ill-tempered healthy eighty-year-old short, stocky woman. Despite her appearance, the woman was physically strong-willed and stubborn. Mama believed in the "old ways" of conducting her business. She deplored technology, especially cellphones and computers. If she had a problem with someone, she would play the telephone game until the last person completed the job. It was her way of not only sticking to her old-fashioned roots, but it was her way of staying off the radar from prying eyes.

"Hugh Schpenus," answered Jenya. He rubbed his clean-shaven face. His pale skin reminded her of the lack of sun the young man had.

She smiled somberly at the tall, muscular man while staring at his bald head.

"How old are you, my dear Jenya?"

Her thoughts still dwelled on her former abated lover, so she used the question to distract her.

"Fifty Mama, fifty," he said dryly.

"Jenya, find this man and bring him here."

The man nodded to the elderly woman, "We found someone in Thailand who came in contact with this Schpenus."

"Good, Jenya," Mama declared. Her voice was suddenly filled with anger, "Bring this man in here," she added while lifting and waving her arm toward her sagging chest.

The man nodded and then stepped out of the office, which looked more like a bar than a professional setting.

Moments later, he returned while gripping the handcuffed man. A mixture of blood and sweat poured down his dark skin and dripped off his afro like raindrops.

"What is your name?" Mama asked coldly while staring at the man's blood lip.

The man looked up at the woman and scoffed. "Lady, I am not telling you a goddamn thing!"

Before the man could speak any further, Mama slapped him hard across his face.

"Do you know who I am?" she asked sternly.

"Yeah," he said as he spat on the wooden floor. "You're some old mean Babushka."

Mama laughed dryly.

"Jenya, where are the plyers?'"

"I have them right here," he replied while giving the woman a heavy set of metal plyers. The cold steel greeted her warm wrinkly hands as she grasped it.

"One last time or else I will pull your little man right off," Mama declared while performing the action of pulling something in front of his eyes, which were wide with fear."

"All right, lady, my name is Cleveland."

"Cleveland, tell me what I want to know, and we will make this easy for you. Where is your friend, Schpenus?"

Cleveland remained silent.

"A pity," Mama said as she placed the plyers on the glass table. Jenya pushed Cleveland, who was on his knees, closer to the woman. "I thought we were coerced. Is this correct in American English?"

"Look, lady, I don't know where he is. The last I heard he was in West End."

Mama smiled, "West End. Spacibo Cleveland."

He chuckled at the woman, "You're welcome, I guess. What are you going to do with me now?"

"We will use you as bait. When this Schpenus shows up, we will kill you both. Jenya, take him back to the basement. Keep him warm with a bowl of borscht.

Chapter 2

Retirement

"Are you sure you want to do this?" I asked.

"Hugh, I have to do this. I am just getting too old for this. Plus, my wife, well I don't have to tell you because…."

I laughed, "Yeah, yeah, I get it. I don't have one, so I wouldn't know." I rolled my eyes. "All right, Stacy, you win. I won't try to keep you."

"Come on," said Stacy while he patted my shoulder. "Let's get one last drink, and that's an order."

I laughed, "You're my boss for one more hour, you know!"

I followed Stacy into the bar. Today was his last day on the job, and it was a long career. Now in his sixties, the man I admired and called my boss was slowly becoming a shell of his former past self. He endured and experienced a crime that I could only imagine. He started out his career in the streets of Detroit and Harlem, New York. Now, in West End, this is where his prestigious career comes to a close.

"So, what are your plans?" I asked after we ordered our drinks. I wanted to throw him a party, but instead, my boss wanted to keep it low-key and private. After all, he wanted to take this opportunity to coax me into considering his position.

"Whiskey, huh?" I said to him, "I never thought of you as a whiskey guy."

After taking a few sips, the man who will soon be my former boss bellowed a laugh, "What did you think I was? A beer guy like you?"

"Hey, there's nothing like a nice cool beverage."

"What kind of beer are you drinking?"

"Old Style," I replied while taking another chug.

My response provoked another laugh, "Old Style? Who are you? An old, retired man at a thrift store shopping for tchotchkes?"

"What key?" I asked after finishing the rest of my beer.

"Tchotchke. You know, the trinkets people buy that only have one purpose."

"And what purpose is that, Stacy?"

"Come on, man, I'll tell you what. Tomorrow, I will be in the office to pick up the rest of my stuff. I have one such tchotchke that you can have. It's an eight-ball. But, not just any eight ball. If you shake it, it'll tell you your fortune."

I laughed, "My fortune, huh? Okay, deal. But, wait a minute, what's the catch?"

He held out his hands as we sat together at the bar. "You owe me nothing, brother. This is my way of showing my gratitude. What you did in Bangkok, and even here in West End, you are one fine detective. And you know...."

I waved my arm, "Forget it, boss. You know how I feel about this. I can't take your job."

"After tonight, we both know it's not my job anymore. It can be yours if you want it. You would make a damn fine commander. Listen to it now, Commander Schpenus. Eh? What do you think?"

I chuckled. It did have a good ring to it, but it just wasn't for me.

"Look," I began while grabbing my second round of beer. "I would love to be a commander, but we both know I would get bored. I love to be out there in the streets, where the action is!"

"All right, buddy, I won't press on this further, but just think about it, okay? For me?"

I nodded and smiled, "Okay, boss, I will. How about I give you my decision tomorrow?"

"Fair enough. I can drink to that," Stacy replied while lifting his glass of whiskey.

Chapter 3

Officer Down

The air outside was cool and calm. A low wind gust greeted us as we stumbled out of the bar. Tonight was a great night to end a long and celebrated history that I shared with my boss.

"Doesn't the air feel cool tonight? What's your favorite season Hugh? Mine is fall because the air just has this certain crisp feeling. Listen," he said to me while we paused in the parking lot. "I want you to seriously consider taking my position. In fact, I already recommended...."

A screeching car broke our conversation.

"Do you know that car?" Stacy asked me.

I shook my head.

A red Cadillac pulled up in front of us.

"Which one of you is Hugh Schpenus?" a man called out in a thick Russian accent. His sunglasses covered his eyes, which was a weird scene since it was two in the morning.

"I am. Why?"

The blonde-haired man flashed a grin.

"Mama says hello!" he said while firing several shots from his revolver at Stacy, who immediately went down.

"No! Boss!" I cried out as the car pulled away like a howling beast.

Stacy fired several shots from his handgun.

"Boss, please stay here. I will get help!"

As I stood up, he grabbed my black leather jacket and pulled me down so our eyes can meet.

"Hugh, listen to me and listen good, you go and get that son of a…."

"Don't move!" the bartender interrupted us as he and several patrons from inside the bar came running out. "I called it in. Help is on the way."

"Listen, Earl, stay with him. I have to go after them," I responded.

Earl the bartender nodded, "Hugh, here," he said while he tossed me his keys. "Take my bike, get those bastards!"

The deep and throaty exhaust notes from the Harley Davidson Evo roared through the night as I caught up to the red Cadillac. Traffic on the freeway was light tonight, which worked in my favor since I had a score to settle.

As the passenger side window rolled down, I aimed my gun and fired several shots at the car. One bullet hit the taillight while the other two struck the right fender. The same Russian man that shot my boss hung the upper half of his body through the open window and returned fire from his revolver.

I had to swerve the Harley to dodge the bullets, which whizzed by me like angry bees. Another shot rang out, hitting the front headlight of the motorcycle. Instantly the headlight was taken out.

Deciding it was time to end this gunfight, I hit the accelerator, causing the engine to roar like an angry monster.

Noticing me coming up fast on their tail, the driver quickly veered onto the exit, barely missing the barrels of water. Together we came down fast on the exit ramp and onto the vacant street. The passenger who shot Stacy stuck his body out from the open window. Before he could fire his revolver at me, I fired my gun, hitting his hand. The man cried out in pain and lost the weapon. My next shot hit the rear tire causing the driver to lose control of the Cadillac.

The car began swerving erratically until hitting a median, causing it to flip upside down, instantly killing the passenger. After stopping the bike nearby, I approached the driver's side of the flipped-over vehicle.

"Get out of the car," I ordered the driver, who was slowly crawling out through the broken window. The loud sounds of crunching glass echoed throughout the empty street. The green glow from the traffic light lit the area like a Christmas tree.

"Don't shoot. I have no gun, see?" the driver pleaded as he finally crawled out of the car.

"Is there anyone else in there?" I asked.

"No, just me. Misha is dead."

I grabbed the driver's brown wool jacket and pushed his body against the driver's door.

"Okay, who are you?"

The Russian man smiled at my question, "My name is Oleg."

"Who sent you Oleg?"

The man vulgarly sent a wad of spit at my face and replied, "I don't have to tell you anything."

After wiping the gross spit from the side of my face, I smiled at him, "Okay, that's fine."

Surprised by my response, Oleg relaxed his body while my left hand held his jacket. With the handle of my gun, I decided it was time to return the favor. I hit his bald head in one smooth motion as if my gun was a hammer.

"Ow! What the hell, man?"

"I am not going to ask you again. Who sent you?"

"Okay, I will tell you. Mama sent me."

"Your mother sent me? I don't understand."

My question invoked an unexpected laugh from the Russian gangster.

"You stupid American. You have no clue who Mama is, but she knows who you are. She wants you dead."

Feeling more annoyed than insulted by Oleg's remark, I threw a punch at his thin face.

"Ow, what the hell? Is this your way of being a nice guy?" Oleg cried out while he clutched the side of his face.

"How do I find your Mama?"

My question invoked another unexpected laugh.

"You idiot, she's not my mama. My mama is eighty years old. This is what we call her. She is in charge of our operation. If you want to find her, go to Russia and find a bar named the Hungry Keeska. Ask for Yuri, tell him I sent you.

Behind us, the approaching sirens filled the night air. I could see the flickering red and blue strobe lights dance around us.

"All right," I said as I turned around to greet the officers who had just arrived.

"Oh yeah, and one more thing," said Oleg. "She has your friend."

I stopped my conversation with the officers and approached Oleg.

"My friend?"

With his back now facing me as the officers searched him for weapons, Oleg turned and smiled at me. "Yeah, your friend Cleveland is it? You better hurry, too, because time is running out."

I approached Oleg, "How much time do I have?"

He laughed, "Two days."

"What happens after that?" I asked even though I knew the answer.

"Your friend dies," he replied while the officers handcuffed him.

Chapter 4

Mercy Medical

It was four in the morning when I arrived at the hospital where Stacy was. The bright fluorescent lights blinded me briefly as I entered. Inside the lobby, there was a mixture of visitors, patients, and guests. Some looked tired, while others looked worried with a color of sadness across their faces.

"I am looking for Stacy. He was in here earlier," I said to the nurse while leaning on the information desk.

"Hugh?" a voice from behind called out.

I turned around to see a fellow detective standing behind me.

"Earl," I began. "Do you know where I can find Stacy?"

Earl, who was in his late fifties, smiled at me and nodded.

"Yeah, but he's not doing too good. He's up on the ninth floor."

"Thank you," I answered.

I passed by a doctor and a nurse who ran by me in a hurry down the ninth-floor hallway. I could hear several machines beeping and buzzing from within the patient rooms as I passed by their open doors.

At the end of the hallway, a police officer in uniform sat in front of the room. Their head was pointed down at the tiled floor while their hands cupped a white Styrofoam cup.

"You're here," the woman said somberly. "He's inside, but be warned, he's in pretty bad shape."

I smiled and silently entered Stacy's room.

A half-filled IV bag hung above him while tubes and a breathing apparatus protruded from his body and mouth.

I let you down, but I will fight and make sure Mama pays," I said while a thick dryness formed within my throat.

The EKG machine began beeping faster, signaling Stacy could hear me. His heartbeat picked up pace after hearing my words.

"I have to go now, boss, but I will be here fighting for you. Just hold on!"

As I left the room, the beeping began to settle, signaling. Stacy felt at ease knowing I was out here fighting for his life and honor.

Chapter 5

Russia

"Where to?" the cab driver asked me. His thick Russian accent filled the small yellow cab, as did the scent of a mixture of vodka and deep regret.

"Take me to the Hungry Keeska," I answered while I searched for the seatbelt.

Upon observing my confusion, the man chuckled coldly.

"No seatbelt, hang on tight, okay?"

"Okay," I replied uncomfortably.

"You look strong enough," he added, grinning through the rearview mirror.

The traffic was quite heavy since I happened to arrive at the heart of rush hour. Blaring hours and clouds of exhaust fumes filled the crisp morning late autumn air.

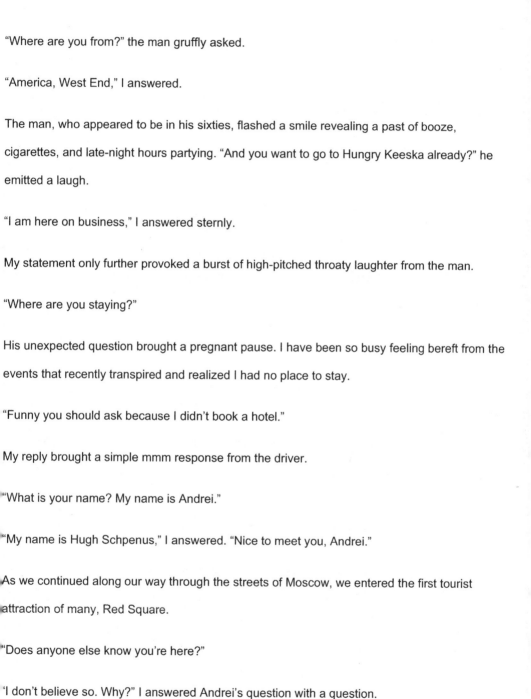

"Where are you from?" the man gruffly asked.

"America, West End," I answered.

The man, who appeared to be in his sixties, flashed a smile revealing a past of booze, cigarettes, and late-night hours partying. "And you want to go to Hungry Keeska already?" he emitted a laugh.

"I am here on business," I answered sternly.

My statement only further provoked a burst of high-pitched throaty laughter from the man.

"Where are you staying?"

His unexpected question brought a pregnant pause. I have been so busy feeling bereft from the events that recently transpired and realized I had no place to stay.

"Funny you should ask because I didn't book a hotel."

My reply brought a simple mmm response from the driver.

"What is your name? My name is Andrei."

"My name is Hugh Schpenus," I answered. "Nice to meet you, Andrei."

As we continued along our way through the streets of Moscow, we entered the first tourist attraction of many, Red Square.

"Does anyone else know you're here?"

"I don't believe so. Why?" I answered Andrei's question with a question.

"Listen," he began while veering the car toward Red Square. "I see another car following us. So don't lie to me."

"Okay, I can get out here if you'd like," I declared.

But, before Andrei could say anything, further gunshots rang out from behind. Bullets dinged off the rear bumper and trunk of the cab.

Andrei began yelling in Russian, which I assumed was profanity from the tone and the glaring look in his eyes as he stared through the rearview mirror. More gunfire rattled behind, hitting the back window while several more shots knocked off his side mirror, causing it to bounce down the street.

"Do you have a gun?" I asked Andrei, who flashed me a smile looking through the mirror.

"It's Russia," he replied. "There are two things everyone has in Russia, vodka and guns." Without further hesitation, he pulled out a large revolver. He began firing wildly at the pursued car while still trying to drive the cab. The loud gunshots rang out like an angry drum as the bullets flew out, hitting the vehicle. For firing out of the driver-side window like a wild cowboy, Andrei still managed to do some damage on whoever was chasing us. The unexpected attack temporarily slowed them down, giving us some time to escape.

"I am going to drop you off here. I can't handle this type of cowboy dermo anymore."

"What is dermo?"

Andrei emitted a squeaky laugh at my question, "What did you say your name was again?"

"Hugh, Hugh Schpenus," I responded.

"Look, I once had a son named Hugh. But he died in a car accident while we were in Austria. I am originally from there, you know."

"That's funny. I am from Austria."

"Oh, yeah? No kidding. Well, look, it's not safe to be out there without a gun," he said while pulling the cab over near the sidewalk outside the giant Red Square area. He tossed the heavy revolver at me as if it were a toy gun, "Take this. It belonged to my grandfather. Treat her well."

"Her? What do I call her?" I asked while inspecting the heavy gun. The bright metal gleamed under the winter sun.

"Anastasia, which was my wife's name. Her name was Anastasia Mungis."

"Are you sure I can have this?" I asked Andrei, who gave me a box containing more ammo. The bullets inside rattled like a box of Tic Tacs.

"Yeah, take it, you will need it more than I will. Now get out of my cab!"

Chapter 6

Red Square

I was still far from my destination since I had no idea where it was. The cold air greeted me as I made my way through Red Square. Saint Basil's Cathedral greeted me with vibrant colors, which glowed under the sun's rays. It was an unexpected sight to see, but I had no time to sightsee. Behind me, loud shouting broke my brief moment of playing tourist. It was the same group from the car, but this time, the three suited men were on foot and running in my direction.

At this point, it was time to find out who they were and what they wanted. I decided to confront the henchmen now that I had a weapon to defend myself with.

"Stop right there! We don't want to kill you or hurt you, Hugh Schpenus!"

Hearing my name caused me to stop walking in my tracks as I faced the three suited henchmen, who each carried an AK-47 assault rifle. Not trusting these nameless strangers, I decided it was time to test their words.

"I don't think so," I said while pulling out the large revolver. It felt heavy but gave me unwavering confidence.

Unsure if I was bluffing or not, the three men stood their ground while the two of the men looked at each other. I could see the uncertainty of my intentions painted on their rugged faces. I held the advantage and it was my turn to show my hand in this poker game of death. With three bullets left in the chamber, I squeezed the trigger hard. The recoil of the gun temporarily pushed my hand back slightly while the bullet shot out like an angry Doberman.

When the three men realized what was happening, my bullet sent the henchman standing in the middle flying back onto the pavement. As his blood painted the plaza the same color as the surrounding buildings, the other two men opened fire from their assault rifles. Luckily, I was prepared, and before the bullets could hit me, I performed a fantastic roll that left me clear of their onslaught.

As I could hear the shots whiz by me like angry hornets, I squeezed the trigger again, causing another shot to rocket out of the long barrel. The bullet quickly found its mark, sending the second of the remaining two henchmen back onto the pavement near my previous attacker, who was still down. With one bullet remaining and no time to reload, I had to make my last shot count.

With the final attacker reloading his weapon, I capitalized on my moment and fired the final round. The bullet shot out and immediately entered the final man's right kneecap, causing him to fall onto the ground while gripping his leg. With the last guy now incapacitated and alive, I reloaded my weapon and approached him.

"Who sent you?" I asked the unnamed man sternly.

He laughed upon hearing my question, "I will never tell you, you stupid Schpenus! You were not supposed to hurt us, but now, we will hurt your friend."

"Where is Cleveland?" I followed up while pointing the now-loaded revolver at the man.

He laughed again and followed by spitting rudely near my black motorcycle boot.

At this moment, I decided it was time to stop playing games with this guy since he clearly wasn't going to tell me what I wanted. I held up the revolver and pressed it against the man's pale-skinned forehead. The barrel indented the center of the man's forehead as he looked up and stared directly into my eyes. His blue eyes showed no fear at the sight of death.

"Do it, Schpenus. I know you won't kill me!"

"Who sent you?"

"Mama sent me and guess what?" he asked while his smile grew wider. The blood continued to stain the gray brick cobbled pavement slowly as his pale hands were painted an oozing blood red color.

"What?"

"She is behind you!"

I allowed a hearty laugh to escape my muscular lungs, "I am not falling for that!" I said while retaining my confidence in my voice. Although, a part of me began to question my words.

"Krasavchik," he said while laughing dryly, "Turn around, idiot. She is behind you."

"Fine, I will play this game," I said while slowly lowering my arm and releasing the pressure from the handgun from the man's forehead.

As I turned around, the barrel of an AK-47 hit me directly at the center of my forehead. My vision became littered with starlight and darkness. So, it turned out the henchman wasn't lying after all.

Chapter 7

Captive

The muffled sound of heavy electronic and techno wave beats brought me back to consciousness. A loud ringing sound erupted loudly as I tried shaking it off. My eyes blinked wide in hopes of regaining my vision, which was quite blurry. Whoever hit me intended to truly knock me out because it felt like I was hit by a locomotive.

The room carried a strange scent, a mixture of menthol muscle relaxer ointment and borscht. I wasn't sure whether to find myself hungry or nervous about being tortured. With my eyesight finally returning, the clarity of my location unfolded. I looked around and saw a long red loveseat in front of me. A gold brass design covered the outer parts of the armrests and the top of the old couch. At the center, an elderly woman wearing a red headscarf sat quietly knitting what appeared to be a green sweater. She paid no attention to me while humming with the Russian folklore music blaring loudly inside the room. Ironically this wasn't the first time I'd found myself in this situation. The instruments strung and jingled loudly, causing my head to erupt like a volcano.

"Who are you?" I asked the woman while noticing a large painting behind her hanging on the peeling gray wall. Pieces of a faded yellow dandelion wallpaper did their best to cover the gray wall. At the same time, this strange painting continued to catch my eye. The flames from numerous lanterns and lit candles danced wildly in the room.

My hands, which were bound, were resting against the armrests of a dining chair. The same gold brass designs felt cold and hard against my arms.

"Mama," she replied softly. "You can call me Mama."

Her accent was a mix of Russian and Austrian.

"Why am I here?" I asked her as my headache slowly dissipated.

She continued knitting and humming away while the music continued playing loud.

Between us, a large coffee table sat with several different colored balls of yarn along with two bowls of what appeared to be filled with borscht. Despite my headache and what I experienced, my stomach grumbled at the sight and odor of the soup. Realizing it must have been numerous hours since my last meal, anything food-related looked good at this point.

"Someone is hungry," she chuckled softly. "Here, eat," she said while a man walked over from behind and loosened the rope that was keeping my arms secure.

I wanted to take advantage of this moment and grab the guard. However, I was still unsure where I was, so instead, I grabbed the metal spoon and ate some of the sweet red soup without any hesitation. It was still warm and delicious.

Seeing me eat brought a smile to the woman's wrinkled face.

"Good my son, eat your borscht. You used to eat it all the time growing up, do you remember?" Her question caused me to almost choke on the warm liquid. Hearing my surprise brought a loud chuckle from the woman. "You see this painting behind me?" she asked while the same man from before poured a clear liquid into my glass goblet, which I assumed was vodka. "This is us, that is you, me, your father, and your brother.

"My brother?" I asked curiously while my voice regained its tone. The sip of vodka helped temporarily quench my thirst.

"Yes, your brother, he is dead. The man standing behind you is Jenya. Don't worry, Hugh, we are not going to hurt you. I only had him tie you up because we did not want you to fall out of the chair." Jenya remained silent behind me. Quickly, I turned my head to get a quick view of what he looked like. Jenya, who wore a red suit jacket and a tight black shirt, appeared to be a tall and bald man who looked like he saw his own share of crime and violence. Scars from previous fights were scattered throughout his face and hands. He was the size of a bulldozer.

"How did my brother die?"

My question brought a heavy sigh filled with sadness and pain from the woman's tiny body, "He died trying to find you. You see, Hugh, we have been looking for you for a long time."

"So, you are Anastasia Schpenus? My mother?" I asked sternly.

"No, I am not a Schpenus. That is your father. I am a Mungis. In our family, it is tradition for you to have my maiden name as your middle name."

"Wait a minute," I said. "You mean to tell me my name is really Hugh Mungis Schpenus?"

The woman smiled wide and nodded, "Yes! You are my Hugh Mungis Schpenus! Oh, my sweet little Schpenus, it has been so long since your Mama has seen you."

This news left me speechless. Here I was, staring at the woman who I haven't seen in over twenty years.

"But papa told me you were dead."

My words caused a heavy frown from Mama's face. "If I ever see your papa, I will kill him! He left me for dead and took you away from me!"

"Where is Cleveland?" I decided it was time to change the subject since this news was overwhelming me.

"That rotten man? He is downstairs. Why?"

"Because he is my friend! I came here to rescue him! Why did you bring me here and almost kill my boss Stacey?"

Mama laughed coldly, "Jenya, bring the rude man up here."

"Listen," Mama began while taking a sip of her goblet. "I brought you here because I am disappointed in you."

"Me? Lady, I haven't seen you in over twenty years, and you are disappointed in me?"

"You killed him!" Mama suddenly yelled while pointing one of her knitting needles at me. "You killed my lover, Phucc Yue!"

"Mama, watch your language!"

"No, you idiot, you killed Phucc Yue!"

I laughed at her ridiculous accusation, "I did not kill anyone. I am a peacekeeper, and I uphold the law! He stole the dragon's talon, which contained the nuclear codes! He is locked away in prison now."

"You are wrong, my little Schpenus. He was killed in prison a few months ago. I blame you for this! And those were my codes!"

I scoffed and abruptly stood up, "You cannot blame me for this. It is unfair! You are not the same Mama I used to know."

The woman frowned her wrinkled face again, "I would say the same about you! No son of mine should be a good guy. Do you think you are saving lives? You destroyed mine!"

Suddenly, Jenya returned with Cleveland, who looked very beat up. The upper half of his body was severely bruised and covered in bloodstains which covered his blue jeans and black combat boots.

"What did you do to him? Cleveland, are you okay?"

Cleveland mumbled something incoherently as he stared down at the wooden floor. I have never seen such a challenging and strong man this broken. Whatever Mama and her henchmen did to this man broke my heart. Before this moment, my friend was a fun-loving man. When we met in Thailand, he talked about friendship and trust.

My fists tightened up and resembled two storms brewing inside me, hate and rage.

"Now, my little Schpenus, it's time for you to prove yourself," Mama declared. She flashed a smile of stained teeth from endless years of torment from constant heavy cigarette smoking and drinking.

"Jenya," Mama called out to him.

The tall Russian man, built like a tank, reached into the side of his inner suit coat and pulled out my revolver.

"Ah, that gun. I recognize this gun." Mama walked over and observed the revolver, "This belonged to your father. I have not seen this in years. Where did you find it?"

I smiled at the woman's question and shook my head, "It was a gift from my best friend, who is also my mentor." Of course, I did not want to reveal the truth to Mama. This left me wondering if the cab driver intentionally picked me up today or even knew who I was.

"I am your Mama. Of course, I know when you lie," the woman said harshly. "I'll give you a choice now, kill this man, or I will kill him, and Alyosha will eat your kolbasa." Mama looked at the center of my blue jeans. Behind us, the loud nails tapped the wooden floor. A large Doberman proudly entered the room. "I can tell you Alyosha is hungry, too, like you were when you woke up. Make your choice, my little Schpenus."

Chapter 8

Choices

Cleveland kneeled before me with his head hung heavy. Sweat dripped from his head and face onto the wooden floor. Beads of blood and sweat rolled down the curves of his muscles. Slowly he lifted his head, and subtly he raised his eyebrow. The revolver felt cold in my hand. The weight of the gun felt heavy, like the decision before me. The crackling flames from the fireplace were the only sound as an uncomfortable silence lingered in the air. I looked at Mama, who stared at me with a strong focus.

I swallowed heavily, knowing what I was about to do would change everything.

"Are you going to do it, my son?" Mama compassionately questioned me.

I nodded, held up the revolver, and aimed at Cleveland without saying anything further.

"I am sorry, buddy," I said to him.

He remained silent despite my apology.

I inhaled deeply and looked at Mama.

"You know what? I changed my mind," I added as I turned and pointed the revolver at the elderly woman. Her facial expression changed from a hardened, fearless woman to one filled with shock and amazement. To see her own son turn against her like a rabid dog left her speechless.

Without any hesitation, I squeezed the trigger.

In concert, Cleveland was now standing with his back facing Jenya. He took advantage of the moment and performed a swift back kick. His boot drove into the bodyguard's stomach like a battering ram slamming into a medieval gate. The feeling from the force of his boot meeting his fat sent the Russian man staggering backward into the ugly concrete wall.

Mama scowled and began yelling in a profanity-laced Russian sentence. I ignored her and continued squeezing the trigger, which emitted clicks from an empty gun. I knew this woman was too keen to know I would never take my friend's life. Although, a part of me wondered if she thought I would have chosen family over friends. But little did she know, my friends are also my family. I would never turn against Cleveland. Next to Stacy, Cleveland is my brother.

"How dare you turn against me! Don't you know who I am? I am your Mama!" the woman yelled as she swung her black cane at me as if it were a sword.

I decided enough was enough. This woman was no mother of mine. With the barrel of the gun in my hand, I smiled at Mama and said, "Mama, chill out!" Then, I threw the gun at her head as if it were a throwing star. The weapon spun wildly through the air, and without warning, the handle slammed directly into her head, instantly knocking her out.

The loud crash caught Jenya's attention as the woman fell onto the coffee table.

"Mama!" the Russian bodyguard yelled out.

Her body laid unconscious on the floor beneath the scattered shards of both wood and glass. The contents within the broken porcelain tea kettle slowly pooled around her headscarf. At the same time, her black wooden, slender cane rested beside her.

This sight further enraged the man, which pushed him over the edge.

"How dare you hurt her! I will kill you!"

The man charged at me like a ravenous bear, but I was ready. I stood firm in my martial arts stance and readied myself for the coming fight. Cleveland seized the moment and began cutting the rope tied around his wrists with one of the shards of glass from the coffee table.

Jenya swung at me with his tree trunk-sized arms, but his attacks were slow. I gracefully ducked and weaved out of the line of fire. Meanwhile, as Cleveland was kneeling over the broken table, the Doberman pounced from behind. It bit down into the left cheek of his buttocks.

"Ow, stupid dog!" my friend cried out as the dog continued to attack him.

I wanted to come to his aid, but I was too occupied dodging the punches from the Paul Bunyan-sized behemoth. My plan was to tire him out, but so far, his display of a never-ending endurance left me in amazement.

With my attention partly distracted by the dog's attack, Jenya's fist found the side of my face. It felt like I was getting hit by a large bag of bricks. The sharply pointed knuckles dug deep into my face like it was a knuckle sandwich. I staggered back as another punch slammed into my head, which left my brain bouncing around like a shaken prized bag containing a goldfish in a child's grip. I held up my hands closer to my face and began my best attempts at blocking the onslaught. Jenya flashed an ugly smile as I continued blocking his punches. I tried to find an opening to counterattack, but he was too fast.

The sound of a dog yelping suddenly broke our fight. In union, we both turned to see Cleveland frantically throwing the shards of glass and pieces of wood at the dog, who was bouncing back and forth barking loudly.

"Shut up! You bit my ass! Stupid dog! Women love to squeeze my love buns! How dare you try to eat the sugar!" Cleveland continued ranting at the dog. "It took me years to shape this butt like a Georgian peach!"

"Leave Baby alone!" Jenya abruptly shouted as he ran over to attack Cleveland.

"Oh, you want some of this, too? Don't you know who I am? I am a black belt in karate fool!" My friend declared while switching his focus toward the large Russian man.

The sound of clattering nails caused me to turn my attention over to the dog named Baby, who decided to run at me to attack. Its ravenous growling and bloodstained teeth were a terrifying sight. It tasted blood and was hungry for more.

"You want some too, dog? Okay, let's dance!" I swung my leg over at the dog that was already in mid-air. With my roundhouse kick in full motion, my boot precisely hit its mark, the side of Baby's slender and muscular body. The surprise counterattack sent the dog flying into a nearby wooden chair.

"This is the leg of thunder! I am the coming storm!" I declared proudly as the dog laid still. "I have subdued beasts worse than you! You have no idea what I have faced, dog!"

"Hey, buddy, when you're done fighting with Baby, how about giving me a hand?" Cleveland asked while still fighting Jenya, who was attacking in full force with a series of punches.

My friend countered with several karate front kicks, but the attacks were futile against an enraged vodka-fueled man.

Without hesitation, I picked up the last remaining unbroken chair, and like a baseball bat, I swung it at the back of the man's bald head. The loud crash of broken wood sent pieces of the chair in every direction. Cleveland followed up with a strong roundhouse spin kick, which connected with the side of Jenya's temple. Our attacks caused the man to topple over like a redwood tree. A clamoring bang rumbled throughout the room, forcing several paintings and candles onto the floor. The flames from the candle ignited the vodka-soaked carpet into a small fire.

"We need to get the hell out of here," declared Cleveland.

Chapter 9

The Heat is On

"We can't leave Mama behind," I said to Cleveland as the fire continued to quickly spread.

"I will grab her, find us some weapons. We are going to need them if we're going to get out of here alive."

"How many?" I asked while tossing an AK-47 over at him.

"A lot. She has a small army. Knowing what took place just now, they will be downstairs waiting for us."

"What's the layout?"

"Outside of that door," he said, pointing the assault rifle toward the only entrance inside the room. "There's a stairwell leading straight down into the dance floor. It's a large open space, several pillars to provide ample cover, and at the front, there's a booth for the D.J. To the left of the dance floor is the entrance to the club.

"Is there a back exit?" I questioned while I loaded my revolver tucking it into the back of my jeans. My white tank top was saturated in a mixture of sweat and excitement.

"Yeah, to the right of the dance floor. I think we should go that way since, knowing Mama, there will be a tank waiting for us if we go out the front entrance."

"A tank?" I exclaimed. "What?"

My question caused a chuckle from Cleveland, who tucked several curved clips into his belt.

"Oh yeah, Mama don't play," he added.

"Okay, I will grab Mama. You lead the way then," I suggested.

"Sounds like a plan, man, but listen, if anything happens," he began.

"No, no, none of this talk," I interrupted. "Come on, let's get out of here."

"That's why I love you, Schpenus man. You are always the optimist!"

I picked up an assault rifle and Mama's unconscious body as I followed Cleveland out of the room, which was engulfed in heavy flames.

"Wait," he said while pausing at the entrance of the room. "Leave the door open."

"Why?"

Cleveland looked at me and answered, "For the dog, man, I love animals, despite this one biting my ass."

Chapter 10

Guns, Lots of Guns

Smoke from the fire behind followed us as we slowly crept down the wooden stairwell. The loud creaks from our weight alerted anyone who was waiting for us.

"Damn, this old stairwell is loud as hell. This is going to give us away."

But despite what Cleveland thought, no one was waiting for us. As we stood alone within the large dance floor, blue, pink, and green laser lights bounced to the sound of silence. There was no music nor anyone around to greet us.

"This feels like a trap," I whispered as I clutched Mama's unconscious body on my shoulder.

Suddenly as if on cue, the loud sound of electronic music turned on. A loud woman's voice filled the room, which was the song was 99 Luftballons, but a fast-paced remix version. It was pretty catchy, but there was no time to dance since all around us, several men appeared. Some wore white tank tops, while others were shirtless, but they all carried heavy, automatic weapons. As the colorful lights bounced off their bodies, I could see tattoo designs of red six-pointed stars.

We quickly took cover behind large white pillars as the gunfire broke out. Bullets relentlessly dinged and bounced off the concrete walls. We both returned fire in every direction while we stayed low.

"Well this sucks," declared Cleveland as he continued firing the assault rifle in the direction of the incoming attacks.

I ignored my friend and fired my AK-47 at a nearby henchman, instantly hitting him.

"Focus on drawing them out, don't waste your bullets!" I advised.

"What? I can't hear a damn word you're saying. This music sucks!" Cleveland yelled through the blaring music.

"I like this song," I added.

Cleveland temporarily ceased his attack. "What? Do you like this song? Why am I not surprised?" he laughed then continued firing his gun.

As more bullets whizzed by, we both continued to take the attackers out. But with everyone that fell, another two showed up with their guns blazing at us.

The rattling and tattering sounds of automatic gunfire reverberated throughout the room. We were facing a small army of henchmen who were only after one thing, rescuing their leader, who began regaining consciousness as she laid beside me behind the pillar.

"You will never get out of here!" she yelled. "Help me! Whoever rescues me will get one million dollars!"

"Not now, lady," I said while hitting her head with the butt of my assault rifle.

With Mama knocked out again, I refocused my gunfire at the incoming army before me. One by one, I shot them while their bullets dinged against the pillar. Chips of concrete fell onto my arms and head.

"We need to get out of here," pleaded Cleveland. "I am running out here. How many clips do you have?"

"I have two, here take one," I answered as I tossed over a clip at my friend.

I fired more shots from my assault rifle. Most of my bullets hit their targets, but this became more difficult. The next song, Rasputin, came on, blaring loudly throughout the dance floor.

"Now this song I like," my friend declared.

"It's quite fitting, isn't it?" I added.

The sound of a heavy shotgun muted the music temporarily with the loud gunfire. Large pieces of concrete broke off from the pillar, sending debris in every direction. The attack left the skeletal wiring parts of the inner post exposed. The gunman stood near me, firing more shots from his weapon.

"I am running out of pillar here!" I yelled while firing at the gunman holding the heavy shotgun. It took a few tries, but I was finally able to bring the attacker down.

"Schpenus, I have an idea!" Cleveland proclaimed. "Slide over that shotgun near you. I will draw their fire and cover you. Head toward the exit! I will cover you!"

I shook my head at my friend while grabbing the shotgun from the nearby gunman's body. "I don't like this idea."

"Trust me, it's the only way, man!" he said, grabbing the shotgun.

"Okay, fine, here, take this!" I shouted as I tossed the last clip for the AK-47.

"Don't worry about me, man, just go!"

I picked up Mama and fired the last rounds from my loaded A.K. while heading toward the back exit. The spotlights and colorful lasers bounced off both me and my surroundings. Not knowing if my attack took out any of the henchmen, I continued toward the exit. Behind me, I could hear a combination of machine guns, assault rifles, and shotguns. Bullets flew by and ricocheted off a nearby banister.

"We're almost there!" Cleveland yelled from behind as he fired several more shots from the assault rifle. "I am almost out of clips here, but it looks like they stopped firing."

I paused and turned around, "Did we get them all?"

"I think so. I really hope so. I am on my last clip here."

Chapter 11

Tanks for Nothing

Suddenly a loud explosion sent us flying back onto the dance floor. Large pieces of the front

entranceway came stumbling forward. The bright sunlight and cold air entered the room,

including a sizable Russian tank, specifically a T-72 tank.

"What the hell?" I cried out while Cleveland and I regained our footing. I picked up Mama, who

was still unconscious, and flung her over my shoulder as if she were a ragdoll.

"We need to get out of here! Come on!" my friend yelled as he fired the last of his bullets from

the A.K. at the tank. The shots did nothing but ding and clang against the heavy armor of the

green camouflaged covered monster. A loud whirring sound echoed behind as the turret turned

to take aim in our direction.

"Oh damn, this thing is going to fire! Get down!" Cleveland shouted as we dove head first onto

the floor. A loud boom broke out from behind us, followed by a large explosion in front of us.

The tank blew out the entire wall, door, and even parts of a nearby pillar. A mixture of concrete

and snow debris blanketed us. Automatic gunfire followed in our direction as we regained our

footing and ran toward the giant gaping hole. A hot stinging sensation sizzled up my leg, but I

paid no attention to it because I knew what had happened. I was shot.

"I got hit in my leg," I said to my friend.

"I think they got me, too," he added. "We don't have time to bleed, come on!"

Outside, the cold Russian wintry air greeted us along with heavy falling snow.

"Great, now where should we go?" Cleveland asked.

But before I could answer, the blaring honking of a horn caught our attention. It was the taxicab driver from earlier. Andrei opened his window and yelled out. "Over here, come on!" He waved us over, and without hesitation, we ran toward him. "Put the old hag in the trunk. I don't want to see that disgusting woman's face," he said harshly.

Without contest, I abided and threw the unconscious woman into the trunk. In front of us, men poured out through the gaping hole with their automatic guns firing out. Bullets shot by, and some dinked off the yellow body of the taxicab. Andrei opened the driver-side window and began firing from his Uzi submachine gun, forcing the army into cover. The gunfire echoed throughout the alley as heavy specs of snow fell onto his green wool jacket and the car's windshield.

We jumped into the back seat, and while still firing the last of his rounds from the Uzi, Andrei shifted the car in reverse.

"Here, keep firing, son," he said, handing me the submachine gun and several clips of ammo.

With the gun accelerating backward down the alley, I opened the window and let loose with the Uzi. Andrei, who had his body turned, was staring out the back window. He briefly glanced over at me and smiled. The fur on his papakha fluttered softly as the cold arctic wind seeped in through the open windows. The tank slowly came out from the gaping hole and slowly turned toward our direction.

"Uh, that thing is about to fire again! You better drive faster, man!" Cleveland yipped while slouching down as the both of us nervously stared at the tank.

Andrei emitted a grunt and said, "Ha, tanks, they are as common as vodka and guns here. Remind me to tell you about the one I have, okay, son?"

Realizing this man was my father, Cleveland's mouth dropped in shock, "Wait a minute, you mean to tell me this man is a Schpenus?"

As we cleared the alleyway, the tank fired loudly from the other end, causing a massive explosion in front of us. The pavement and building were heavily damaged from the attack, but luckily, we were okay.

With one graceful turn, the small yellow sedan spun around completely.

"Damn, you're one good driver, Mister Schpenus!" Cleveland added in amazement.

Slowly the gunfire behind us faded as we drove away from the alley and the Hungry Keeska. We were finally free from danger.

Chapter 12

Like Father Like Son

"Try not to bleed to death in the backseat, okay? It is costly to get blood out of the seat. This is my office."

"Where are we going, father?"

With the sun hastily setting before us, we sped through the streets of Moscow.

"The airport, I have contacts waiting for us with a private jet. He will take you to America."

"Okay, who are your contacts?" I asked.

"Oleg and Pasha. I know Oleg very well. He saved me many times during the war."

"Which war was that, sir?" Cleveland inquisitively asked.

"Your friend here, he asks a lot of questions. Very nosey," Andrei answered, which felt more directed at me than Cleveland.

"Well, okay, a touchy subject, I get it. Look, man, I just want to thank you for saving us back there."

Andrei grunted and replied, "I did it for my son. I will do anything for you, Hugh. You know this, right?"

"Yeah, I do, father. Thank you."

This was the first time in a long time that I had seen the man whom I looked up to (other than Stacy) flash a smile.

As the sun hid behind the horizon, Andrei took off his hat and tossed it onto the passenger seat. Cleveland fell asleep, and I continued thinking. There was so much I wanted to say to Andrei, but I wasn't sure where to begin. I had many questions, like how he ended up here in Moscow driving a cab. But deep down, I knew he wouldn't open up to just anyone because of his hardened tough dad mentality.

"Son," he abruptly said, causing me to lose my thought. "I have to tell you something." He slowed the vehicle down as we rolled into the entrance to the airport hangar. The squeaky brakes, along with the thumping from the trunk, woke Cleveland from his nap.

"Ah, your mother is awake," my dad added as the three of us exited the vehicle. "Here, take this," he said and handed me a small thick envelope. "Open this later. It will explain what I wanted to say to you."

"I don't understand, father," I said sadly. I already knew he wasn't going to come along. In the distance, a snow storm started to pick up. Through the blizzard, I spotted several approaching vehicles, including three tanks.

"Looks like we are out of time," Andrei declared. "Get your mother and get out of here. I will hold them off."

Just then, Oleg and Pasha approached us with their guns drawn.

"This is Oleg," my father said while shaking the man's hand.

"We need to get in the air now," Oleg said. He was clean-shaven from head to toe and well dressed in a clean suit. He was built like a small tank because I knew he would give me a good fight if we ever went down that path. Pasha, on the other hand, was much taller and thinner. He also wore a nice suit, but something seemed strange about him. Unlike Oleg, Pasha made no eye contact with us.

"You must be Pasha," Andrei said while opening the trunk to the taxicab. "And this is my wife who you know as Mama. Take this ved'ma out of my sight and away from here. I don't ever want to see you again."

"The feeling is mutual, sobaka!" Mama retorted.

"Look, before you two lovers get hot and heavy, we need you two to say goodbye," Cleveland stated sarcastically.

"Goodbye, Ana."

Mama shot a wad of spit at Andrei's face, "You haven't seen the last of me!"

"I disagree, Ana. I am going to die protecting our son. Get out of here, Hugh."

I wanted to interject and plead, but the stern look in my father's eyes made me reconsider. It would be an insult to argue like a child with a man who is about to sacrifice his life for me.

"I love you, father," I yelled.

"I know, and I do, too, my son. Now go!" Andrei shouted as he picked up an enormous bazooka along with a large, heavy machine gun. "I will hold them off as long as possible."

Together, we entered the private jet. Mama begrudgingly took her seat across from me. At the same time, Pasha and Oleg entered the cockpit to give the orders to the pilots. Cleveland tied the cranky elderly woman down in her seat while I stared out the window from the jet. I could see my father waving us off as the army approached from afar.

Gunfire broke out and rattled through the cold night air as the jet went down the runway. I could see my father take cover behind the taxicab in hopes of drawing their gunfire. A giant rocket shot out from within the hangar towards one of the three approaching tanks. Instantly one of the tanks exploded. Cleveland joined in and watched the action unfold as the jet engines began to power up. The loud whirls from the twin engines were loud enough to almost drown out the gunfire. Bullets dinged off the sides and wings of the sleek white jet, but the hull was thick enough to withstand their gunfire.

Heavy machine gun fire erupted from inside the hangar taking most of the approaching army out. The tanks were still focused on taking us out as both of their turrets fired in unison. Luckily, we had begun our takeoff, and instead, two large explosions rang out where we were shortly before. As we finally soared into the night sky, a large explosion erupted from inside the hangar.

Chapter 13

The Letter

Moments later, a strange and ominous calm filled the cabin. We were finally clear of danger and out of Russia, but something felt unsettling. Oleg sat in front of me staring out the window through his sunglasses while Pasha sat across Mama. Their eyes were strangely locked together as if they were speaking to one another.

"So, Oleg," I began. "How do you know Pasha?"

Oleg pushed up his shades and looked over at Pasha, then at me and said, "I have known Pasha for five years. One day I was drinking at a bar, and he was seated beside me. He said, 'Hey you, you know where I can find work? I am a boxer and good with knives.' Ever since then, he's been helping me out. Why do you ask Hugh?"

"How long until we arrive in West End? I don't know about you, but I need a nap!" Cleveland added while closing his eyes.

"We should arrive in America in twelve hours. Take a nap, all of you. Pasha and I will keep an eye on Mama."

Suddenly the lights within the cabin dimmed. Even if I wanted to fight it, I could not since my eyes closed from feeling heavy. The calming sound of the jet flying through the sky brought an uncomfortable sleep, not because of the hard, brown leather seats, but because I knew something was amiss. I thought about everything that transpired on the last day. It was tough losing my father, considering I spent barely any time with him. I was unsure who he really was the first time, but it made sense now that I've thought about it. He must have been waiting for me to arrive at the airport. And somehow, he knew I was being followed from the moment I had set foot in Moscow. But who tipped him off? That was the question lingering in my head.

Five hours later, a strong wave of turbulence broke my sleep. I opened my eyes and groggily looked around. Oleg appeared to be asleep with his head hung forward while Cleveland snored loudly. Pasha was not in his seat, but I assumed he was in the toilet. Meanwhile, Mama was fast asleep with her head tilted back and her mouth open as drool hung from her wrinkled chin.

I reached into my pocket and pulled out the envelope my father had given me. Unsurprisingly enough, the letter consisted of a single page. Inside, I found a photo of my father and I during our last fishing trip together. I was holding up a large fish as a kid while my father, who was sporting a white tank top and a thick 1970s trademark mustache, was smiling proudly beside me. The letter was short and peculiar.

Son listen to me carefully. I am sorry I was not there for you through these years. I know what you did in Thailand. It made your mother very angry, and I thank you for this. That bitter old woman does not deserve to be happy after what she's done. She stole everything from us. I need you to promise me something. No matter what happens in life, and no matter how tough the situation, you will never give up and will always keep fighting. You are my son. You are a Schpenus.

P.S. – Do not trust anyone but Oleg.

"Everything okay?" Pasha asked as he returned to his seat.

I abruptly looked up and folded the letter, then stuffed it back into my pocket.

"Yeah, everything is just fine. How are you?"

Suspiciously Pasha tilted his head and smiled at me, "I am fine, thank you." His voice and demeanor were calm and focused.

Without saying anything further, I stood up and entered the toilet. After locking the door, two little lights turned on. It felt like an awkward office more than a restroom. Everything was neat and clean as if the facilities were not used, which was strange since Pasha was here before me Knowing Cleveland and Oleg were both out there with Mama and Pasha, I quickly washed my hands and face. I needed to think of a plan.

I stepped out and returned to my seat when I noticed Pasha was staring out through the window at the night sky. His reflection made me wonder if he was focused on my every move.

"What time is it, Oleg?" I quietly whispered. Behind me, Cleveland continued snoring loud. Oleg sat motionless in the same position when I woke up. His head hung forward while his hands were peacefully clasped together. "Oleg?" I repeated.

"I don't think he can hear you," answered Pasha.

"Oh, and why is that?" I asked curiously.

"Why don't you check on him?" Pasha sardonically added while he still focused out through the window.

I cautiously approached Oleg while the plane subtly rocked from the sudden spat of turbulence.

"Oleg? I quietly called out as I reached out to tap his shoulder. Through his black suit, his body felt cold and stiff. "Oleg?" I called out again, but his lifeless body fell forward onto the green-carpeted floor this time. A small dagger stuck out from the back of his neck, along with a long line of dried red blood. It appeared the man had been dead since shortly after takeoff. Pasha must have silently assassinated him while we were all asleep.

Before I could say anything further, the assassin moved swiftly and placed a small blade against my throat.

"Now, let's make this easy, shall we? Wake up your friend over there. It's time to free Mama."

Chapter 14

What Goes Up

"What are you planning? I asked Pasha, who held the knife against the center of my throat.

"Shut up! Hey you, man, wake up!"

Cleveland slowly opened his eyes only to see me standing at the center of the aisle with Pasha directly behind me with the knife pressed against my throat.

"What the hell is going on here?" my friend asked as his eyes grew wider, realizing this was not a dream.

"Pasha killed Oleg and is threatening to kill me, too, unless you untie Mama."

"Okay, man, whatever you say," Cleveland said nervously as he held out his hands. "I will untie her now."

As he stood directly across from us, I stared straight into Cleveland's brown eyes. I slowly winked my eye, signaling for him to be ready.

"Give me one of your knives," he suggested to my Russian captive.

Upon hearing Cleveland's statement, Pasha arrogantly emitted a laugh.

It was at this moment that I decided to capitalize and seize my opportunity. With one swift move, I lifted my head back into Pasha's face, causing him to loosen the knife from my throat. Blood poured out profusely from his now broken nose.

"Ow! That hurt!" he cried out as he dropped the small knife.

The plane hit another abrupt spat of turbulence, causing the three of us to lose our footing. Pasha took this moment to counter my surprise attack.

"Enough of this! Untie her now, or I will shoot both of you!" he ordered, aiming a handgun at both of us.

"Okay!" I said. I held the handle of the small knife downward and pressed the blade softly against my wrist. "Cleveland, untie Mama now."

"All right, I got you, man. I will untie her now," he said.

Awakened by the commotion, Mama surveyed the room and noticed the knife in my hand.

"Pasha look out!" she cried out as I ducked down and threw the knife forward. Pasha carelessly fired two shots that went directly into the cockpit door. As my blade struck into Pasha's heart, he fired another shot in our direction, which carelessly rang out and struck Mama in the head. I was unsure if this was intentional or accidental, but this left the woman I called my mother dead.

"Damn, he shot her square in the head," declared Cleveland.

But before I could take in the moment, the small jet suddenly dipped forward.

"Whoa! What the hell is going on?"

"The plane is going down!" I yelled. "We need to get out of here."

"Oh no, those two shots must have hit both of the pilots! We need to get out of here!" Cleveland frantically yelled.

"Pasha has some good aim because I am not sure if this was all intentional or not," I added.

"Whatever the reason, I am not ready to die! There are so many babes I need to see in Thailand. I can't die yet, Hugh Mungis Schpenus!"

I shook my head at my friend, "You know if it was anyone else, and if we were not about to die, I would object to that name!"

Cleveland laughed, "Yeah whatever, man. Come on, let's find some parachutes and get out of here!"

Together we moved forward toward the cockpit gripping the top of the hard, brown leather chairs. A loud whirring sound echoed through the cabin as the plane continued its heavy descent.

"They must be in here!" Cleveland proclaimed as he opened a small closet. "Yes! I found…"

"Yes, you found?" I asked while making my way toward his side.

"One. There's only one parachute, man. What do we do? Flip for it?"

I shook my head and said, "No man, take it. Get out of here!"

"No man, that's crazy talk! You take it!"

"Cleveland, just take it, but promise me something."

His eyes began swimming in a pool of tears.

"Please promise me something."

"For you, anything man," he finally said.

"Go to West End and tell Stacy you will take his place. He is resigning."

A heavy and short silence fell between us. "All right, man, I will do it. But what about you?"

"Don't worry about me! I will think of something!" I said as he locked the parachute securely around his body. "Now, get the hell out of here before I change my mind!" I sarcastically stated.

Cleveland opened the side door causing a heavy depressurization of the cabin. "Are you sure you will make it?"

I smiled at my friend's words, which held a regretful tone. "Yeah, man, don't worry about me! I am a Schpenus, I will find my way out of this situation. No matter the situation, we always find a way out."

He took one last look at me and then jumped out of the falling plane.

The air was cold and heavy. Cleveland pulled the strap, causing the chute to burst open, which drew him upward as if he were on a giant kite. In the distance, the jet plane continued its descent into the ocean. As it crashed hard into the raging waters below, a bright yellow flame rose high up into the night sky, followed by a loud explosion.

"Damnit, Hugh, I hope you made it out of there alive!" Tears rolled down the man's face as he landed safely in the water.

Behind him, the loud foghorn from an approaching freighter caught his attention.

Chapter 15

The End

The rain fell hard as the large crowd stood huddled beneath the black umbrellas. Lightning flashed silently as the priest offered a moment for people to pay their respects.

Cleveland, dressed in a flashy brown suit, approached the makeshift podium.

Before he began, he surveyed the crowd of mourners who sat in the white metal chairs in hopes of seeing his friend. A part of him hoped this was only a temporary loss, but another part of him told him it was nothing more than wishful thinking. The rain slowed and trickled off the chairs and umbrellas. He cleared his throat and began.

"I am not sure many of you know this," he cleared his throat again and smiled briefly. "But Hugh Schpenus's full name is actually Hugh Mungis Schpenus." Several quiet snickers and whispers could be heard throughout the crowd. "Many of you knew him as a tough cop who took great pride in his job to protect each and every one of us in this great city. But I knew him as more than just a cop. I knew him as my best friend. If I could say one word to describe Hugh, it would be courageous. He gave up his life just so I could be given another chance," he paused and looked at Stacy, who sat still in his wheelchair. Paralyzed from the waist down from the failed assassination on his life, the former chief of police smiled proudly at Cleveland. "I am taking that chance to be the best, but I know I have some pretty big shoes to fill. Stacy, you were a mentor and even a second father to Hugh. I also hope to have that same honor and privilege to say the same about you. Finally, West End will never be the same without you, Hugh."

Cleveland cleared his throat again to fight the tears forming within his eyes. A lump hung heavy in the back of his throat. "We may have lost a fine good cop, but West End lost a best friend."

The empty casket was slowly lowered into the ground, followed by bagpipes being played in the background. It was a somber scene.

Days later, Cleveland leaned back in the black leather chair. It was a strange feeling to be sitting where his mentor, Stacy, used to sit. Being the head honcho gave the new chief of police a peculiar sense of conformity compared to the wild and crazy life he experienced in Thailand. He smiled contently. This was the complete opposite of that previous life, but he promised a friend an oath he swore to keep.

"Sir," the young woman said while standing at the entrance to his office. "Here is today's mail," she said with a smile while gently placing a small stack of envelopes on Cleveland's desk.

"Thank you, Miranda," he answered as he sifted through the mail.

Something peculiar caught his eyes. It was an envelope with no return address. He perked an eyebrow and wondered what it was. He held up the envelope beneath the light to see the contents inside, but the envelope was too thick.

He carefully opened the envelope only to see nothing more than a photo slide out. It was a picture of a scrawny young boy holding a large fish and standing beside him was his father, who looked like a harsh but stern and caring man. Cleveland smiled and turned the photo around to see the initials A.S. and H.M.S.

Made in the USA
Las Vegas, NV
08 March 2022

45271372R10075